TREASURE HUNTERS

The Treasure

E. A. HOUSE

EPIC Escape

An Imprint of EPIC Press
abdopublishing.com

The Treasure
Treasure Hunters: Book #6

Written by E. A. House

Copyright © 2018 by Abdo Consulting Group, Inc.

Published by EPIC Press™
PO Box 398166
Minneapolis, MN 55439

Printed in the United States of America.

Cover design by Laura Mitchell
Images for cover art obtained from iStock and Shutterstock
Edited by Ryan Hume

Library of Congress Cataloging-in-Publication Data
Names: House, E.A., author.
Title: The treasure/ by E.A. House
Description: Minneapolis, MN : EPIC Press, 2018 | Series: Treasure hunters; #6
Summary: The San Telmo: a Spanish merchant vessel lost in a hurricane off the coast of
Archer's Grove while carrying a magnificent dowry home to the Spanish princess. Chris,
Carrie, and Maddison think they know where it is. But if they want to find the ship, they're
going to have to survive screaming caves, psychotic oceanography professors, dangerous cave
floors, and ghosts.
Identifiers: LCCN 2017950431 | ISBN 9781680768817 (lib. bdg.)
| ISBN 9781680768954 (ebook)
Subjects: LCSH: Adventure stories—Fiction. | Code and cipher stories—Fiction.
| Family secrets—Fiction. | Treasure troves—Fiction | Young adult fiction.
Classification: DDC [FIC]—dc23
LC record available at http://lccn.loc.gov/2017950431

*For archivists, college professors
and park rangers*

*Forgive me for taking liberties
with your professions.*

CHAPTER ONE

WHEN THE WOMAN FROM REDD'S TELEVISION show turned up at the police station, clutching a black three-ring binder and looking deeply uncomfortable and slightly jumpy, Michelle Grey didn't even bother to ask. She just took a moment to remember the woman's name from the first time they'd met—Bethy Bradlaw, if she remembered correctly—and then waved her over to the desk where Robin Redd was sitting with his head buried in his hands, next to the Kingsolver cousins and the McRae girl and her father. Then Michelle went back to tracking down a boat using the impression of a key left in plaster.

But she didn't forget they were there. A very long career in law enforcement had given Michelle an excellent ability to pay attention to what was happening behind her, and the loss of one eye hadn't hindered that skill. So, when Redd skimmed three papers and stopped dead on the fourth, Michelle didn't even bother to put the phone down—she was on hold with the second-largest boat store in Archer's Grove—before she said, "That had *better* not be one more clue to that ridiculous treasure."

Redd froze. Bethy bit her lip guiltily, and McRae, who had been trying to read what Redd was reading over his shoulder, stifled a hysterical laugh. Michelle sighed. Then the blasted Starside Marina finally answered their phone—how many calls did a boat shop regularly get on a weekday morning, anyway?—so she didn't quite catch the furious conference that went on while an apologetic woman at the marina explained that they didn't carry a line that would correspond to that key. She hung up just as Bethy Bradlaw said, "Well I'm not *lying* to the Federal Bureau of Investigation!"

"Lying about what?" Michelle asked.

"Err," Redd said.

"It's . . . " Bethy Bradlaw started, and then trailed off. "To be honest I don't know what any of this means, I just don't think it's any good." She offered a single sheet of vellum paper to Michelle, who took it and frowned at a page of ornate but mostly legible handwriting. It was in Latin, which Michelle could vaguely recognize from a handful of church hymns but couldn't actually read.

"It's a page from the journal of the missionary priest who built the *Santa Maria Estrella del Mar*," Redd said.

"And that means?"

"He writes on this page about the sinking of the *San Telmo*," Redd explained. "'Against the high cliffs where the mussels grow so thickly.' This is— this is enough proof of where the *San Telmo* ended up that you could get a dive crew together and they wouldn't all think you were crazy."

"I see," Michelle said. What she was actually seeing was a terrible vision of all the subjects of interest in her investigation disappearing on another treasure hunt, only to get attacked by the still-at-large Griffin somewhere with no witnesses. That man had the most irritating habit of finding the Kingsolvers when nobody expected him to and an equally bad habit of disappearing before the police could get there. It was, well, irritating. If Griffin would just once try his shenanigans when the police or the FBI were in the area—wait.

There was an old saying about how if the mountain won't come to Muhammad, then he'd just have to go to the mountain. Detective Hermann had been following up on some leads that had evaporated in light of the key Redd and McRae had found, which meant he was free right now. Catching his eye and hopefully conveying "Forgive me for volunteering you but I think they'll accept you faster than me" with her gaze, Michelle turned to McRae and made a decision.

"If you do decide to go off looking for that boat a second time, I'm going to insist that you bring Detective Hermann along with you," she said, and McRae blinked once, slowly, then turned to Redd and shrugged.

"It's not going to bother me," Dr. McRae said, "but I don't have a boat."

"Oh, I can get a boat," Redd said cheerfully. "And a scuba diver, since I have one in my address books."

"Is this a reliable person, or someone who bought a certificate off the internet?" McRae and Bradlaw asked in unison. Then they turned startled gazes on each other, while Redd folded his arms and declared that she may have been certified in Ohio but she *had* taken all the necessary tests and classes.

"It might mean fewer people try to shoot me," Chris Kingsolver suggested to his cousin Carrie and Maddison, Dr. McRae's daughter. Chris was sitting in between the two girls; they punched him in the shoulder in unison.

It was only after they had left, with McRae assuring Detective Hermann that they would call him before they did anything at all suspicious or even slightly dangerous, that Detective Hermann turned to Michelle with a sigh.

"Really?" he asked.

"I can go if you don't want to," Michelle said. "Or we can send Forrest, he has a romantic streak and he might enjoy looking for a lost treasure ship."

Hermann glanced pointedly at Forrest, who was happily charming a description of a boat that might possibly match the key out of one of the same receptionists who had hung up on Michelle for wasting his time. "Though . . . it looks like he's doing good work here," Michelle said, then added, in a disgruntled undertone and mostly to herself, "I come across as a little harsh on the phone."

Later, she would learn that at that point Detective Hermann was manfully restraining himself from mentioning that Father Michaels had described her as "a woman with a voice admirably suited to yelling through a bullhorn, who incidentally has a missing eye that makes her steely glare all the more impressive" before he'd even met her. Instead, the detective simply gave Michelle a slight smile and reassured her that he really had no objection to shadowing the treasure hunting and keeping an eye out for Willis Griffin.

✗ ✗ ✗

They reconvened at Carrie's house, for the simple reasons that her living room was bigger than Chris's and Maddison's and both her parents were at work. Although Carrie did call and tell them she was having some friends over and even put Dr. McRae on the phone to reassure her mom.

And anyway, it was nearly noon, since they'd been stuck at the police station for some time while Agent Grey looked as though she was getting a migraine, and they were hungry. Carrie's dad had just been complaining the other day about needing to get rid of leftovers, so in Chris's mind it was perfect—they could do Carrie's dad a favor. True, Chris didn't think he really meant that he wanted a television star to finish off the ham, but he also hadn't *said* that he didn't, so . . .

At that point, Carrie cut him off by whacking him over the head with the rye bread. This effectively ended Chris's guilt-trip, plus it squashed half a loaf of rye, which wasn't even supposed to be out of the refrigerator. Carrie and Dr. McRae were making everyone a ham sandwich apiece, and nobody in their right mind put ham on rye.

"I like ham on rye," Redd offered, leaning against the kitchen counter and nibbling on a carrot. Chris was not at all sure where he'd found the carrot, and very sure he didn't want to know.

Dr. McRae thought Redd had terrible taste, and when Redd pressed the issue, McRae started making threatening gestures with the plastic deli bag containing the sliced ham. Chris decided that retreat was in order and took himself out of the kitchen to go spread Carrie's notes on the location of the *San Telmo* across the living room coffee table.

Professor Griffin had, to Chris and Carrie's absolute bewilderment, returned all of Carrie's books to the public library sometime after he threw her overboard—*all* the books—plus all of Carrie's notebooks, still in the book bag she'd originally packed them in. Chris did not see why the professor couldn't have done the same for his backpack—he'd been quite fond of that shirt with the purple turtles, for one thing—but finding Carrie's books and notebooks had been an unexpected piece of luck nonetheless. All of Carrie's research had been in that book bag, and if the professor had thought to look through Carrie's notes he might not have been so confused about where the *San Telmo* lay hidden, a location that the fragment of journal they'd just found only seemed to back up. "Against the high cliffs where the mussels grow so thickly" didn't have that many interpretations if you were talking about Archer's Grove. But why had this piece of the puzzle been missing for so long, and what had it been doing in the Edgewater Archives?

Chris didn't realize he'd been talking out loud until Bethy, who had also fled whatever terrifying things were going on in the kitchen, said, "I don't know. I was trying to find a picture of Richard E. Emanate." She sat down on the couch with a sigh, and added, "And I just realized I never even got the picture I was looking for."

"It might be available in one of the online collections," Dr. McRae offered as he carried over a large plate of ham sandwiches. "The local photos collection in particular is almost a complete inventory of archival holdings, especially if they've been . . . um. . . " He trailed off. He was standing in the archway that separated the kitchen from the living room, frozen with the sandwiches balanced precariously. "What?" he asked, looking from a startled Chris to Bethy, who was trying to look up the archive's online collection on her phone. "It's my job to know this sort of stuff!"

"I sort of assumed you were learning all this from scratch," Chris admitted, rather than saying something to the effect of "I didn't expect you to be competent in this area, too," or "the Richard E. Emanate Collection was Aunt Elsie's pet project because she loved all the manatee-shaped notepaper he used."

"I used to work in an archive before I finished my degree," Dr. McRae explained, finally setting the sandwiches down very carefully next to the page from the journal. "This looks like it could come from the Archive's own Mission Church Collection," he added, picking the piece of vellum paper up by one corner. "And it's *been* well preserved for some time, there's no recent discoloration, even if this edge has been folded."

Which put a hole in Chris's first theory, which had been that someone had been reading through the diary and had ripped out a page when interrupted and then hidden it in a panic.

"I just want to know what it was doing in that folder in the first place," Bethy said absently, squinting at her phone. Dr. McRae put the piece of vellum paper down on the coffee table and sighed.

"I would guess . . . "

"You would guess what?" Redd asked. He had a potato chip on his head, even though the bag of chips Carrie was holding had not been opened yet; Chris was not going to ask about that either.

"I would guess that Elsie was being careful," Dr. McRae said, reaching for a sandwich. Maddison joined Chris on the couch, and then they were all assembled in the living room, although Bethy was still frowning at her phone and possibly trying to look up Richard E. Emanate. "Elsie could put together the faintest of connections and make the most amazing conclusions but she absolutely hated going off heresy and half-proof," Dr. McRae continued. "If there were three different ways to corroborate where the *San Telmo* went down she'd use all three just to get the most accurate idea of— Robin, did you put *jam* in these?"

"Only some of them?"

"I look away for *one second.*" Dr. McRae put his ham sandwich down and gave it a dubious look. "Anyway," he said, "odds are, Elsie just happened to be going through the Emanate papers and the Mission Church Collection at the same time. I know she was worried about something—about someone," he amended, "so when she realized that she'd found something more about the treasure, she might have decided that hiding a page that mentioned the *San Telmo* in the wrong box was more important than original order."

"Original order?" Carrie asked, looking up from her attempt to scrape peach jam off a slice of bread.

"The original order the papers were in when they came to the Archive," Dr. McRae explained, peeking inside a second sandwich. "Most archivists think it's a good idea to preserve that arrangement if at all possible because it might tell you something about the person who made the papers, or what that person thought about the papers they were storing." He put the second sandwich down—he'd taken only a bite out of his first one—and turned to Redd. "Only *some* of them?" he asked, clearly irritated.

"What do you have against peach jam?" Redd asked.

"It doesn't belong on ham sandwiches!"

Carrie met Chris's eye and shrugged. "We were out of mustard?" she offered, which didn't go very far in explaining why Redd had decided to put peach jam on the sandwiches. Unless jam and mustard were related condiments, as far as Redd was concerned, which was really the most reasonable explanation and still meant that Chris was not going to enjoy his own sandwich very much.

"It's not that bad," Maddison offered, as her dad dissected his own and Redd's sandwich in a quest for two slices of bread without peach jam on them. Carrie was frantically rescuing her notes from the resulting stickiness and Bethy had started on a second sandwich when the doorbell rang.

"I'll get it," Chris offered when nobody else seemed to notice.

Carrie's family had a very open-plan house, at least in the front; the front door led into the living room, which opened up into the dining room, which led into the kitchen, which simply meant that when you opened the front door you could see who was on the front porch all the way from the kitchen. Chris knew that, in the same way he knew that the antique diving suit his uncle had once bought at a thrift store and steadfastly refused to get rid of was always going to live in the spot between the television and the bookcase. *And* in the same way that he knew that that diving suit—which was one of those bubble-headed ones with lots of rivets and brass trimming—was always going to terrify the unwary. He'd never thought of the problems with the way the house was laid out, at least not how it might be dangerous for someone to open the door and be immediately visible to the entire rest of the house. Especially if, say, they happened to be somebody who really shouldn't be at Carrie's front door.

In Professor Griffin's defense, Chris realized afterwards, he must have thought Carrie's parents were home but Carrie wasn't yet. As it was, Professor Griffin had launched into an "I just managed to get the ship into port and I've been so terribly worried about the kids" speech while blinking back tears before he stopped and realized who he was actually talking to and said, "*Chris?*" sounding both horrified and shocked.

"You," Chris said, at a loss for words. Did Professor Griffin truly believe Carrie's parents would fall for that? They'd been the ones Harvey had called, for heaven's sake!

"Me?" Professor Griffin asked, and if he was aiming for offended he missed it by a mile from sheer nervousness. Chris and Professor Griffin might have stood frozen in the doorway stammering at each other for the rest of the day—which would have been okay, as the professor might otherwise have actually used the gun Chris only belatedly realized was tucked into the professor's waistband—except that the front of the house was open and everyone who had been sitting around the coffee table could see exactly who was at the front door. And apparently, Dr. McRae had a bit of a temper when you pushed him too far.

"*You!*" Dr. McRae snarled, and then to the shock of Chris (and Maddison if the way she yelped in alarm was any indication), Dr. McRae lunged at Professor Griffin. In doing so he sent the entire couch, and Bethy, who'd been *on* the couch, flying.

"Whoa, hey, Kevin, there's no need to do anything rash," Professor Griffin said quickly, trying to back out the door without turning his back on anyone, just as Redd grabbed Dr. McRae by the back of the shirt and they both fell over a side table and knocked the diving suit over with a huge crash. Chris, at a loss for anything else to do and still the person closest to Professor Griffin, slammed the door in the man's face. He was just petty enough to hope that he'd catch a couple of the professor's fingers in it, but he had no such luck. Then there was a moment of shocked silence, broken only by Carrie quietly talking to the 911 operator, and Redd patting Dr. McRae awkwardly on the head and pulling him to his feet.

"I *hate* him," Dr. McRae said to the house in general. He started to kick the fallen diving suit but gave up halfway through the swing and ended up just poking it with his foot.

"I know, but you really mustn't go around attacking all the people you don't like," Redd said. "It always ends badly. Especially if the other person has a gun. And it makes the police irritated and producers angry and Bethy sigh."

"Oh no, I'm fine," Bethy offered, popping up from behind the upended couch and shoving it upright with great effort. "I just had the wind knocked out of me. And I found a couple of quarters and a whole bunch of hair bands back here."

"So, that's where they went," Carrie said, and then blushed furiously when everyone turned to look at her, at which point Chris finally realized that he had been in terrible danger yet again and sat down in order to wail, "Why me?" more effectively. Counting the time someone broke into the house, the time Bethy's brother had a nervous breakdown, and now this little incident, Chris had been menaced with a gun three times to Maddison and Carrie's two. And nobody seemed terribly surprised!

"Because you have an admirable amount of curiosity?" Maddison finally offered.

"If I get voted 'most likely to get shot' when they put together the yearbook next year I'm blaming you guys," Chris said.

✗ ✗ ✗

Of course, by the time the police that Carrie had so sensibly called got to the house, Professor Griffin was long gone. Detective Hermann said a few dire things along the lines of "Of all the times to cut the police surveillance off . . . " But then he turned to Chris and said "Slamming the door in his face was still the smartest thing you could have done" very sternly but approvingly, so it could have been worse.

"It's not like I go around trying to get myself in trouble," Chris said. Detective Hermann just raised one eyebrow and looked at him, which, since Chris was trying to prop the diving suit back into its customary corner, was not at all helpful. Chris was only now discovering that the thing was twice as heavy as it looked and that the helmet made it very top heavy. It was also worryingly possible that the detective had finally coaxed the full story about what had happened in the state park out of someone—possibly a worried Carrie—and was now laboring under the delusion that Chris was prone to getting shot at and held hostage.

CHAPTER TWO

DETECTIVE HERMANN REFUSED TO GO AWAY after fingerprinting the front door and checking the street for suspicious tire tracks, citing Professor Griffin's consistent stalking of the Kingsolvers, and the fact that nobody could tell which direction he'd disappeared to or if he had come on foot or not, as proof that an officer needed to be on the scene. "And since Agent Grey so *sensibly*"—he rolled his eyes slightly—"suggested I accompany you on your treasure hunt, this seems a good enough place to start as any," he said. It was impossible for Maddison to tell if he was being sarcastic or not—Maddison *could* guess that Agent Grey had thrown Detective Hermann under the bus by volunteering him, and Agent Grey herself had been radiating guilt when they'd left the station earlier that morning—but Detective Hermann seemed to be taking everything in stride, even the ham-and-peach-jam sandwiches and the fact that according to Helen Kinney, the probable location of the *San Telmo* was legendarily haunted.

"Yeah, that's where the Screaming Caves are," Ranger Kinney said matter-of-factly via Skype on Carrie's laptop, which was nestled on the kitchen table amongst Carrie's research notes on the *San Telmo* and every single one of the books Carrie had used. She seemed blithely able to ignore the groans of disbelief and horror that followed her pronouncement. Once the introductions were out of the way—Helen Kinney had never actually met either Chris or Carrie, although she had, on seeing Carrie for the first time, squinted and then mentioned that she'd done an elementary school presentation with their aunt once—Carrie had obligingly held her marked-up map to the computer screen and Helen had immediately known the area.

"The Screaming Caves," Maddison's dad said flatly. He'd made himself a ham sandwich without any peach jam over Redd's offended protests that he made perfectly good sandwiches, but he wasn't getting very far in eating the sandwich because he kept having to stop and look alarmed. First at Redd for eating a ham-and-peach-jam sandwich, but then at the sheer number of books Carrie piled on the table, and now at the admittedly alarming news about the caves.

"It's just an old superstition," Helen said, waving a hand impatiently through the air. "Someone or something expired in those caves once upon a time, and their restless spirits have haunted the area ever since. Hence the screaming. Heaven forbid we remember that that area of the island gets a nice volume of wind year-round and that wind blowing through caves makes a nice, eerie howling noise."

"But does it make a *screaming* noise?" Bethy asked, scribbling frantically in a notebook.

Helen glared.

"What?" Bethy protested. "This is great! This is local color! And *I* know it's picking at semantic details, but that's the sort of thing that makes a good sound bite."

Helen sighed. "The Screaming Caves—the Six Screaming Caves, if you want to be specific, although most people only count five—are on the absolute most remote tip of Archer's Grove. Building there has always been difficult because the limestone is crumbly and the amount of natural erosion is tremendous; and for roughly the same reason the soil is too sandy to make for good farming so it's *never* been heavily populated."

And suddenly Chris realized something. "Father Gonzales is supposed to have spent the rest of his life—after he witnessed the *San Telmo* disaster, I mean—trying to help the souls of the drowned.

Because he had been so badly shaken by *hearing them crying out in torment*," Chris said excitedly.

"So . . . ?" Helen asked, but Carrie's eyes had lit up.

"So, that could be a reference to the Screaming Caves!" she said. "I can't believe I didn't think of it before; it did seem weird that he could have heard people screaming over the storm that must have been raging at the time."

"The caves were doing it for them," Maddison offered darkly. "No wonder nobody wants to go near them."

"So, if a treasure ship was going to lie forgotten and overlooked for untold generations, then that's a good place for it," Maddison's dad said.

"Oooh," Bethy said, writing furiously. "That's a good point too."

"Well, I guess," Helen said, "but there was a USGS survey team out there in the fifties doing pretty in-depth terrain mapping and they didn't notice anything at all, and someone walks the one road through that part of the park before we open the area every year, it's not *completely* remote."

"And you're sure that the USGS survey team was actually a USGS survey team, and not a team from the CIA looking for Cesar Francisco?" Bethy asked.

"No, but if they *were* a CIA team they also did a bang-up job on the geological survey and were immensely passionate about the silt in the mussel beds," Helen said, voice as dry as the Sahara Desert. "My point, if you would all stop interrupting to be sensational, is that you're heading off to go poke around the most unstable and remote part of the island, so you need to be *careful*. And for the love of all little green growing things," she added as she signed off, "don't mess with the plants or wildlife!"

"Why did we call her again?" Redd asked Maddison's dad.

"So we don't go charging into a national park blind and get ourselves killed by angry mussels?"

Maddison did not point out to her dad that, angry as mussels might get, they were highly unlikely to attack people. The offhand comment had made Chris start in surprise and frown as though he were thinking, and if the danger of attack mussels was enough to keep Chris Kingsolver from getting into some kind of trouble, Maddison would just as soon let him believe it.

The qualified scuba diver met them at the marina. Her name was Maria Sanchez, and she possessed a motorcycle, and this was a huge relief to Maddison's increasingly frazzled dad, who nearly went insane trying to work out the logistics of stuffing seven people into one car. It was the first hurdle to searching for the *San Telmo*, or at least the first hurdle of the day—after a round of phone calls to Chris's parents, Carrie's parents, Maddison's mom, Agent Grey, and the mysterious qualified scuba diver, they were more or less ready to go and more or less not going to disappear and scare anybody. Funnily enough, the only ones worried were Carrie's mom and dad, who were shopping at the grocery store and understandably puzzled by the news that they needed to buy a new jar of peach jam. Chris's mom *did* sound suspicious but she didn't ask any questions, especially since Chris managed to imply that he was going to see about a job interview while he was out. Maddison's mom sighed so deeply everyone could hear it even though the phone wasn't on speaker, and Agent Grey just grumbled that they had better not fall overboard this time. "She must not be having much luck with the boat key," Detective Hermann said.

And apparently, Maria Sanchez would just park her motorcycle at the marina and meet them with her gear in front of the *Meandering Manatee*.

Maria proved to be small and cheerful, with her pretty dark brown hair in a very tight French braid and a compass rose tattooed on one ankle. How, precisely, she knew and liked Robin Redd was a complete mystery; she didn't seem nearly crazy enough.

"Now that is a very long and very complicated story," Maria said, when Bethy asked the much politer but roughly equivalent question of how Maria knew Redd. "He was taking a filmmaking seminar at a college in Ohio, I was working at a scuba-diving shop in Columbus. We met in a rock quarry . . ."

"Quarries are about the only place you can go scuba diving in Ohio," Redd explained, which made a surprising amount of sense. Then he introduced everyone to his boat, a sneaky move that very effectively prevented any more prying into the "long and complicated" part of how he had met Maria by giving them all something to be very horrified about.

"Okay," Maddison's dad said. "I had some reservations about you coming across as the crew of a *haunted* ship but now I buy it. Redd, that is hideous."

"I'll have you know I spent a lot of money on

that manatee," Redd said, gesturing to the large inflatable purple manatee dangling from the hook most people would have used to hang a wind sock. Bethy looked down at the video camera she was packing along, looked up at the manatee, and sighed heavily. "It was money well spent," Redd protested.

"Stop while you're only in a little bit of trouble," Maria told him, clapping him on the back. "Now come on, let's all go get seasick from something other than this ship's color scheme!"

"Oh no," Chris said, horrified, just as Carrie produced a bottle of Dramamine from her backpack and tossed it at him.

✗ ✗ ✗

The journey to the most deserted tip of the island was relatively quiet. Detective Hermann pulled Maddison's dad and Redd aside to ask them some questions, and Bethy spent the time filming the shoreline and talking quietly with Maria. Chris managed to fall asleep, proving that the red-and-purple-painted ship might actually have mysterious powers, and Carrie got quieter and quieter as they got farther from the marina.

"Something the matter?" Maddison finally asked her. Carrie jumped; she'd been leaning against the railing, gazing out at the horizon.

"No, not really," Carrie said. "I was just thinking . . . we were almost here last time we, well, you know." Maddison nodded. "All Professor Griffin needed to do was turn the coordinates around and he would have found the caves we're looking for," Carrie said. "He came *this close* to finding them."

"And that's scary?"

"Actually I think it just makes me really mad," Carrie said. "Why did he wait this long to go looking, and then why does he keep giving up so easily?"

"So, you'd rather he was a more *persistent* thorn in our side?" Maddison asked.

Carrie sighed even more heavily and dropped both arms over the side of the railing. "*Noooo*," she said. "I just wish he'd commit to something and quit stalking around in the shadows. I hate guessing what he's up to." She flicked a piece of peeling paint into the water, and then added in a much quieter voice, "And I really wish I knew why Aunt Elsie knew all this and didn't go after the treasure herself."

"Maybe she was trying to keep it out of Professor Griffin's hands?" Maddison offered. "She obviously knew that he was up to something, or at least she suspected he was up to something. She *did* leave you and Chris that note and send my dad a warning."

"Hmm," Carrie said.

"Or maybe she already found it?" Maddison suggested, chipping away at a peeling piece of paint as well.

"What?"

"Maybe she already found it," Maddison said, warming to the idea. "If your aunt was as good at puzzles as everyone is always saying she was, then maybe she put all the puzzle pieces together and actually *found* the *San Telmo*."

"But then why wouldn't she tell somebody?" Carrie asked. "Why keep the archeological discovery of the year a secret, especially if she suspected Professor Griffin of being up to something? The *only* way we're going to be able to *stop* Professor Griffin is to get to the *San Telmo* first and then prove that we've found it first."

Which was why they'd all so quickly agreed that they needed to bring Bethy and Redd and a video camera along, and why it looked as though Chris was going to get the shaky handheld-camera-footage feature film (or at least documentary) he was always pining over.

"Well . . . " Maddison bit her lip. It *was* just a theory; she hadn't exactly hammered all the holes out yet.

"I can actually answer that," Redd said behind them, and Carrie and Maddison both jumped almost a foot in the air.

"You can explain why Aunt Elsie might have found the *San Telmo* but never told anyone about it?" Carrie asked dubiously when she came back down to Earth.

Redd opened his mouth confidently and then paused, a pained expression crossing his face. "Well, when you put it like that I should amend the statement," he admitted. Carrie crossed her arms and glared at him, tapping her foot. "I have a possible explanation," Redd said.

"Which is?"

"We swore a blood oath in college," Redd explained. Maddison's dad sighed so heavily it was clearly audible even though he was inside the ship's cabin putting on more sunscreen. "And now that I say that out loud it doesn't make as much perfect sense as it did when I was thinking it over inside my head."

"Robin," Maddison's dad said, poking his head around the open door with a sunscreen-white nose, "we were eighteen- and nineteen-year-olds, it wasn't . . . " He sighed. "Just because we swore that we would all stand in front of the wreck together before we ever revealed its existence to the world doesn't mean that Elsie remembered that promise all these years," he said gently. He laughed, without any humor, and added, "Willis sure didn't."

"Well, I'm not Willis Griffin," Redd said. "And you aren't, either. So tell me, Kevin, would you have announced that you found the *San Telmo* without calling any of us? Because I sure wouldn't."

"I . . . no," Maddison's dad admitted. He rubbed distractedly at his nose, sneezed at the sunscreen, and sighed. "No, I would have tracked you all down if I found the *San Telmo*. Jeez, I'd have tracked you all down if I found a good *clue* to the *San Telmo*."

"So, Maddison's theory is more than a theory?" Carrie asked. "It's what both of you would do?"

"Yes," Redd agreed. "But of course I was never quite as astute as Elsie was so I probably wouldn't have realized there was someone dogging my tracks, which throws any theories based off me out the window. I'm hardly a good indication of what Elsie would do in a given situation."

"Well, if we take the exact opposite of what you would do in any given situation, *that* might give us an idea of what Elsie would do," Maddison's dad suggested.

But his eyes were dancing. "The same could be said about *you*, Kevin," Redd retorted.

Maddison figured that whatever well-worn college memories they might have dredged up, they weren't *too* bad. Then Chris startled awake and demanded to know why Maddison's dad and Redd were sort of arm wrestling on the deck, and they had to explain the whole thing all over again.

Come to think of it, what exactly did Redd mean by "blood oath"? Had there been pricking of fingers and signing of names in blood?

✗ ✗ ✗

Brad was miserable, tired, frustrated, and uncomfortable, in that order. Or any order. The point was that he was having a terrible time. The hotel room he was currently holed up in—a two-bed sort of deal in the most unappealing part of town and at the very cheapest rate—was the most horrifying example of its kind Brad had ever seen, and Brad was *not* a man accustomed to the finer things in life.

The floor was peeling yellow linoleum, the overhead light had been flickering erratically ever since Brad had turned it on, there was a mysterious stain creeping out from under the bed, and the air conditioner was a window unit that made a lot of noise while doing nearly nothing to the temperature in the room. The air in the little room was stifling with humidity and smelled of mold and damp, and the bedspreads had a peculiar damp and gritty feel from being saturated with that humidity. But the true source of all Brad's misery, discomfort, tiredness, and frustration was seated *on* the horrifying bedspread of the adjacent bed, turning a piece of yellow paper over and over in his hands with a faraway look in his eyes. Brad was more than a little thankful for that faraway look. Professor Griffin was much more terrifying when his attention was focused on the present with Brad, instead of on the sticky note he had taken from the Kingsolver girl and still seemed to think was a useful clue.

He was terrifying just sitting there thinking, anyway. Brad had been looking for a way to ditch the professor since the evening before, when the man had dragged Brad into his office on the college campus and smashed his own statue of Melville after an exhausting day of avoiding what looked like a state-wide manhunt. But the smashed statue had simply been the professor's way of retrieving a key to the boat he hid in an out-of-the-way marina on the far side of the island, and Brad had been on that blasted boat before he could make a break for it. Then Professor Griffin had driven the boat around the island all night with some sort of maniacal skill, staying just one step ahead of Coast Guard patrols and the eventual police and then even an *FBI* presence. They'd docked the boat at yet another out-of-the-way marina, this one clearly involved in some very shady dealings, before hiking cross-country and into the very outskirts of town, where the professor had rejected three different hotels before settling on this one as the least conspicuous.

Aside from occasionally muttering to himself about "her"—whoever that was—the professor had done the entire thing in perfect, unnerving silence, save for when he gave Brad brief directions. And once inside the hotel room he had pulled that yellow sticky note out of his pocket and lapsed into silence yet again, this time while staring at the paper as intently as if he wanted to catch it on fire with his eyes. He'd held it up to the flickering fluorescent light; peered at it cupped in his hands; closed his eyes and rubbed it thoughtfully between his fingers like he was looking for secret writing that wasn't there; and even brought it to his mouth twice as though on the verge of eating the thing before thinking better of the idea. Brad had by this point come to the conclusion that Harvey had absolutely had the right idea by running away at the first opportunity. No amount of money was worth dealing with a crazy guy, and no amount of money was worth dealing with a crazy guy who didn't seem to realize he was crazy.

What Brad *did* know, all the way in his bones the way he had always known when a situation was way more dangerous than even a gun could handle, was that this Willis Griffin guy was only going to get worse, and that if Brad hung around he was only going to have worse and worse trouble.

He was just starting to talk himself into bolting for the door—he'd noticed the convenience store across the street when they came in, and if he could just get inside he could probably get the cashier to call the police for him, and then if he played his cards right he might get preferential treatment from the police for turning Griffin in—when Griffin suddenly sat bolt upright.

"That's it!" he said.

"What's it?" Brad asked nervously. Griffin had turned the piece of yellow paper around so that it was upside down and he had his head tilted at an uncomfortable angle. Any farther to the side and Brad would have begun suspecting demonic possession. Not that he was ruling that out yet.

"Here I was, thinking it was a mistranslation or a wrong number or an off calculation or a coded message," Griffin said, clutching the paper to his chest. "But all the time it was a transposition!"

"Err," said Brad, who wasn't entirely sure what transposition meant.

"Transposition, my dear man," Griffin said, "means to switch things around, to reverse, to, oh, etcetera!"

Brad nodded, even though he still wasn't sure what the guy was going on about—apparently he had figured out where the ship he was looking for had sunk—because Griffin was slightly less scary when he was happy. Case in point, the professor leapt off the bed as if he hadn't been sitting in the same position for two hours, and then strode out the door, beckoning imperiously. "Come on, we've got to beat them to it," he announced, and Brad grabbed his sweatshirt and wallet and followed reluctantly, casting a longing look at the convenience store as they plunged back into the woods. It was too far away to make a break for it, and then there was that small wrapped case the professor had paid the owner of the second marina for. Brad was *not* in the mood to find out if it held a gun.

CHAPTER THREE

"Okay. So, the *San Telmo*—what are you hoping to find?" Bethy said, swinging the camera from the green blur of the passing shoreline to focus on Chris. Her voice was professionally steady and clear even though her expression was screaming "Why am I here and why am I doing this?"

Redd and Dr. McRae had agreed, with Detective Hermann, that a filmed record of the second search for the *San Telmo* was a very practical idea. Unfortunately, they couldn't fit the entire film crew of *Treasure Hunter* on the *Meandering Manatee* and still have room for the detective and both Chris and

Carrie, so in the necessary absence of a film crew Bethy had been drafted. Bethy was nervous because she had a technical idea of what to do behind the camera but had only ever filmed once before, at her niece's birthday party.

"So the audience's expectations are a little different," she'd said while arranging Chris in front of the nicest section of the *Meandering Manatee*'s deck. Of course Chris had never been on camera before, so he was nervous too, and there was still the distinct possibility that this film was going to accidentally record something that had to be admitted to court and so would never see the light of day anyway. Detective Hermann had explained that at length before Bethy had started filming and before wandering over to the railing so he could look longingly at the fish that were occasionally drifting by. He was, apparently, fond of fishing in his very infrequent spare time.

"Well, according to legend," Chris said when Bethy waved the hand not holding the camera at him in a "go on" gesture, "the *San Telmo* was loaded down with twice the amount of gold the other ships in the 1717 fleet were carrying because it was the ship honored with bringing the Princess of Spain's dowry back home."

"Princess Annamarie," Carrie added, poking her head in.

"Yeah," Chris said. He resisted the urge to push her off screen, mainly because he had no idea how far to push. "And the crown princess was said to be extremely fond of gold and of flowers, so the one thing everyone who goes looking for the *San Telmo* really wants to find is the gold crown that was intended for the princess."

"And why is that?" Bethy asked.

"It's supposed to have been made in the shape of a flower crown, using the princess's favorite flowers," Chris explained. "There was a merchant who described it in a letter to his sister as being so lifelike it was as though the hand of Midas touched it, it was supposed to be so finely worked that you could

see the individual flaws in each of the daisies . . . "
Chris trailed off. A very strange thought was nagging
at the back of his brain.

"Thanks, Chris," Bethy said, because she was a
very kind person who didn't keep filming while you
were having unsettling thoughts. "I'm going to go
corner Redd and get to the bottom of this dratted
manatee."

"Good luck," Chris said absently, and then went
and cornered Dr. McRae in the poky little cabin
while Carrie made distressed faces at him.

"Was my aunt's favorite piece of treasure from
the *San Telmo* the princess's crown?" Chris asked
Dr. McRae, who didn't look startled by the question at all, although he did jump a little when Chris
asked him—he'd had his head in a cupboard.

"Yes, it was," Dr. McRae mumbled through
a bite of the Pop-Tart he had been looking for,
rubbing his head where he had whacked it on the
cabinet in surprise. "She was really phenomenally
good at making flower crowns herself and she always

said that a solid gold one would be really neat. Why do you ask?" He looked ever so slightly nervous.

"Because I was curious," Chris said slowly, "and because I knew Aunt Elsie liked flowers but not how much she liked flower crowns—wait, that was you!" Dr. McRae jumped again and choked on the mouthful of Pop-Tart.

"What was me?" he asked, while Carrie tried to stomp on Chris's foot.

"You—you were the one leaving flower crowns on Aunt Elsie's grave!" Chris said as a dozen different little things suddenly added up.

"Well," Dr. McRae said, "um, well, I was . . . but I wasn't the only one!"

"I was leaving *flowers*," Chris said.

"So was I," Carrie added quietly. "And so was Redd—"

"I didn't do it!" Redd yelled from out on the deck. "At least I don't think I did it," he added, poking his head into the cabin. "What am I supposed to have done?"

"You left flowers at Aunt Elsie's grave," Carrie said.

"Well, of course I left flowers at Elsie's grave. What kind of jerk goes to a funeral without a flower arrangement?"

"Okay, then maybe it wasn't you. I was talking about *after* the funeral," Carrie said.

"Oh, I did that too," Redd explained. "Couldn't find the asters I wanted for her before the funeral so I had to come back."

At which point Detective Hermann started laughing helplessly over the railing, but all they eventually managed to get out of him was that there had been a sudden and unexplained fad for asters that the local florists had reported to the police as a trend in need of careful monitoring.

✗ ✗ ✗

"What do I think about the *San Telmo*?" Detective Hermann asked Bethy in response to her asking him the same question. "Well, I think it would have been a good idea to tell the detective investigating the case about the maybe-haunted, possibly cursed, definitely dangerous ship everyone was wandering around trying to find *before* Willis Griffin descended into madness trying to plunder it."

Unlike Chris, who she'd filmed against the wall of the cabin so his hair didn't clash too terribly with the paint job, Bethy had positioned the police detective against the bright red railing of the *Meandering Manatee*, chasing everyone else either into the ship's small cabin or around the opposite side of the deck. She had a good eye for the dramatic and the visually striking, and Detective Hermann looked appropriately detective-like, framed against the sparkling blue ocean and the ship's railing with the least terrible paint job.

Chris was watching from a safe distance because filmmaking interested him and it was a great opportunity to get everyone's perspective on the *San Telmo* without anyone noticing him listening in.

Maria was sketching Redd's inflatable manatee as it spun lazily in the wind, Carrie had cornered Dr. McRae to talk about the coordinates of the *San Telmo*, which were fast approaching, and Maddison had applied a layer of sunscreen and then fallen asleep in a pool of sunshine on the other side of the ship.

"So, do you think the ship is haunted?" Bethy asked. She'd asked everyone that question, along with "Do you think the ship is cursed?" as well as "What do you hope to find when we unearth the *San Telmo*?" and "How long have you known about the sunken ship?" By listening in on Bethy's interviews Chris had learned that the majority opinion was that the *San Telmo* was not haunted, that the eight people on the boat were evenly divided on the question of whether it was cursed, that Carrie had an encyclopedic knowledge of the treasure that was supposed to have gone down with the *San Telmo*, and that Robin Redd had read a storybook about the sinking of the *San Telmo* when he was five that had stuck with him throughout his life. Chris couldn't help wondering what sort of parents Redd had and if they were perhaps responsible for some of his strangeness. Who read books about tragically sunken ships to their kids as bedtime stories?

True, Aunt Elsie had. But that, Chris would maintain stubbornly if anyone pressed him, was an entirely different matter.

"Do I think the ship is haunted?" Detective Hermann sighed. "I think it's haunting *me*, if that counts." Bethy laughed. "Yes, you can laugh, but this has been the strangest case I've worked since the monkey-smuggling ring. And I'll have you know, Bradlaw, that *I* did not spend my early teenage years trespassing in national parks or looking for missing treasure ships. The closest I ever came was in Glee Club—yes, really—when we learned a sea shanty that happened to mention the ship."

"No," Bethy said incredulously, as Chris sat up and blinked. *Glee Club*? "There's a song about the *San Telmo*?"

"There's a folk song about long-lost ships," Detective Hermann said. "And I just now realized that the *Saint Elmo* they mention in the refrain is really the *San Telmo.*"

"Well, then, let's hear it," Bethy said.

"Oh, no. I'd rather tell you about the monkey-smuggling ring, and I swore on my luckiest coffee mug that I'd never tell a living soul who wasn't on the case what happened that night."

"Well, you could always do both," Bethy offered.

"There's really a song that mentions the *San Telmo*?" Chris asked, curiosity getting the better of him. Detective Hermann sighed. Then he clasped his hands in front of him and took a deep breath.

"I don't remember the whole song," he explained. "But there *is* a traditional folk song called 'Lost Forever' that mentions a *Saint Elmo* that sunk off the coast of Florida, and, well, see . . . " He lifted his voice.

"'For they've found the *Katie Mary*, and they've found the *Boris Lee*,'" he sang, "'but the ship they called *Saint Elmo*, she still lies beneath the sea. Now her rigging's strung with seaweed, and her anchor's made of sand, and the men who called her deck their home, died far from solid land, hmmm hmm, hm hmmm hm . . . hm . . . hmmm' . . . *Aaaaand* I don't remember the rest." He was blushing slightly but there was no reason for it. Detective Hermann, it turned out, had an excellent singing voice. Chris had to fight down a natural impulse to applaud.

"That was really good!" Bethy said, saying what Chris was thinking. "Do you do theme songs?"

"Do I do—" Detective Hermann abruptly realized what Bethy was planning and rolled his eyes. "I am not doing a theme song for *Treasure Hunter*," he said firmly. "Your show doesn't have a theme song with *words*. It's just a minute and a half of enthusiastic drums with clips of Redd falling off things in the background."

"Ah, but little do you know that Redd actually wrote words for the theme song," Bethy said, balancing the camera on a rickety deck chair so she could rummage through one of her file folders. "We've just refused to let them see the light of day because he tried to rhyme cucumber with nuclear."

"Nuclear and cucumber?" Detective Hermann whispered, brow wrinkled.

"Wait," Chris said, "how do you know what the theme song for *Treasure Hunter* is, anyway?"

Detective Hermann clammed up, which was very unfair.

✕ ✕ ✕

There was both Scottish and Irish in the McRae family genealogy, although for some six generations neither side of Maddison's family had laid eyes on the home country. But the Irish insisted on persisting in a stubborn streak of red hair and blue eyes, which had cropped up in one of Maddison's cousins this generation but had skipped Maddison's side of the family entirely. In Maddison, the genetic red-headedness meant that she came from a family with a tendency toward pale skin that burnt easily. So falling asleep in direct sunlight was probably the last thing Maddison should be doing.

But the sun was warm without being scorching, and Maddison was running on a sleep deficit from too many long nights and odd hours chasing the secrets of the *San Telmo*, and the gentle rocking of the waves against the boat was so soothing, and before she quite knew what she was doing she was dreaming.

Maddison wasn't one of those people who always remembered her dreams, and she also wasn't one of those people who could never remember what she had been dreaming about after she woke up. In fact, aside from one especially terrifying nightmare about sand coming to life and eating people, she'd never really worried about her dreams. True, Maddison had poked her nose into enough books about ESP and remote viewing that she had a healthy respect for how little human beings understood about what their brains did while they were sleeping, but her own dreams tended to be so simple and boring and easily explainable that Maddison had never much believed in prophetic dreams, or even that you could psychoanalyze yourself through your dreams. Dreams just *were*, and usually hers were especially unremarkable.

This time, she dreamt about boats and water, and a guy only a few years older than her with dark hair and a silver ring on one hand, who needed to tell her something but couldn't be heard over the waves and the gulls.

The weird thing was the sense of urgency that was completely unconnected to anything that happened in the dream. Maddison felt like there was something very important hovering just out of her reach, whispering at her, and when a spray of cold seawater startled her awake it was that sense of pressing urgency that took the longest to fade.

"Pleasant dreams?" her dad asked, offering Maddison a hand and hauling her up from the deck. It hadn't been a detailed dream to begin with and the images were already starting to fade, so Maddison shook the last of her unease away with the last shreds of the dream itself and shook her head.

"Just dreaming about boats," she said lightly, ignoring the way that sense of unease was trying to come back. It was just a random dream, and anyway she didn't even know who the guy in her dream was.

Which should have been a warning sign right there, because Maddison never had dreams about people she didn't know.

✗ ✗ ✗

The coordinates Carrie had so painstakingly put together and then so desperately tried to preserve led them to one of those little out-of-the-way spots that travel magazines call "hidden wonders" and thereby ruin through exposure. The raggedy edge of Archer's Grove's unstable limestone sort-of cliffs plunged down to meet a little half moon of a bay, the beach where they met a pretty white sand that gave way to thick grasses and dark trees. The tideline looked like it came in almost to the feet of the grass, and the limestone cliffs were riddled with holes and caves. It was wild, and surprisingly desolate, and as Detective Hermann observed grimly, very far from a police presence. It was also difficult to get the *Meandering Manatee* in close to the shore without beaching her in the surprisingly shallow waters; in the end they had to drop the anchor and wade in to the beach, which was how they discovered that while the sand *looked* pretty, it was coarse and rough on the feet, and they kept kicking up broken bits of mussel shell. There weren't, however, nearly as many mussels as Chris had expected, what with the mussels having been an important clue to the location of the ship. When he mentioned this Carrie just sighed.

"Development wrecked their habitat," she explained. "And the resulting changes from erosion didn't help. The mussels Father Gonzales wrote about like deeper water and less sun, so you don't find them on this beach anymore except as shell fragments. There are a couple of protected areas farther up the coast, though." So at least they weren't disturbing the habitat of an endangered species while looking for the *San Telmo*.

"This sand must all have come from the white limestone in the cliffs," Maria said as they splashed to shore, her mask in one hand and air tank in the other. "You can see that the cliffs are almost exactly the same color as the sand, and there must be a lot of erosion when storms blow up. Look at those caves!" She sounded delighted.

"Scuba divers," Maddison's dad said with the sort of sigh he usually only reserved for people who had been driving him nuts for a very long time.

"Oh, this is going to be *fun*!" Maria said in response. "Where's your sense of adventure?"

"Well, all my friends said I left it behind in a well the last time I went treasure hunting," Maddison's dad said, and then Redd choked violently on air and had to be pounded on the back. Bright red and shamefaced, Maddison's dad said, "That was maybe not the politest way to put it. Too soon, huh?"

"I wasn't going to *say* anything," Maddison said, shocked despite herself. Maybe her dad wasn't as okay with this whole mess as he seemed. She shared a worried glance with Carrie, who must have been wondering exactly the same thing Maddison was. Could they actually finish this without everyone losing their tempers and getting into another fight?

"It was a cistern," Chris grumbled under his breath. "A *cistern*, not a well."

Or the natural level of goofiness Maddison's best friends possessed would get them through this. *Way to focus on the least important point, Chris*, Maddison thought.

The sand didn't get any softer when they made it to the beach. In fact, it got worse, because the sand on the beach was both coarse and hot from the sun. Maddison was wearing sandals that she hadn't taken off underwater but her dad did a small dance of pain before he found a rock to sit on while he put his shoes back on.

"So, now where?" he said as he tied the laces.

"I don't know," Carrie admitted, sitting down on a piece of driftwood. Chris was thoughtfully burying his feet in the sand. "The latitude and longitude point actually comes to right in the middle of that cliff over there"—Carrie pointed—"and I just realized I was expecting the point to be in the middle of the ocean and that we were going to send down *Moby* to check out a wreck on the ocean floor." Which couldn't happen now because the beloved submersible was back at the local college, and Maddison had heard that what was left of the oceanography department had *Moby* under strict lock and key so the submersible couldn't disappear again. Professor Griffin's actions had the entire college in a state of panic, and nobody had time for the renegade professor's friend's niece and nephew. "So, now I can't even tell if we're in the right place," Carrie finished.

"Oh, we're in the right place," Chris said suddenly. He was grinning, a delighted and only slightly manic grin. "There are pieces of eight washing up on this shoreline."

CHAPTER FOUR

DR. MCRAE HAD BROUGHT ALONG A METAL detector. Under different circumstances Chris might have found this the tiniest bit suspicious— why did he have a metal detector in the first place, if he had given up treasure hunting for good?—but Chris was far too excited by his discovery of a piece of eight to complain about a piece of equipment that made treasure hunting easier. And he'd already figured out that Dr. McRae might have *tried* to leave treasure hunting behind him but you could never really get it out of your blood. Case in point: Dr. McRae not only had a metal detector, he also had a plan for mapping the beach out in a grid so they could graph where they found something and catch any emerging patterns. The only thing he didn't have was graphing paper, and Bethy was in the middle of pointing out that they could just sketch it out on a piece of paper or even use a smooth spot on the beach when Carrie produced several sheets of graphing paper from a Ziploc bag that also held pens and a sheet of acid-free paper. Sometimes Chris's cousin was the weirdest thing in existence, and that existence had included gun-wielding maniacs and ghosts.

With the aid of the metal detector they found a shockingly large pile of old coins. They also found a big handful of regular old pennies and quarters, a Canadian penny, a pound coin, a button, the remnants of a box of fishing tackle—Redd narrowly avoided finding several of the hooks that went with it by stepping on them, but Maria yanked him out of danger just in time—and a car key.

"It would make so much more sense if this was

a boat key," Chris said as Dr. McRae finished a second sweep of the beach. Carrie and Maddison had a highlighter and were studying the map hastily drawn on a piece of graphing paper and Chris had flopped down on the beach next to them to poke at the pile of found metal objects. "Who drops their car keys into the ocean?"

Maddison giggled over the map. "Well, I have this cousin with more dramatic flair than common sense who *threw* her car keys into the ocean in the middle of a fight."

"Oh, are these hers, then?"

"No, my aunt actually made her go get them back," Maddison said. "Aunt Ruth is kind of scary when she's mad."

"Yeah, and you know what else is scary?" Carrie said, capping her highlighter and spreading the crude map over a convenient rock. "*This.*"

There was a pattern to where they'd found the coins. Especially after Carrie had tossed all the modern coins out, along with the car keys and the fishing tackle. This left her with only the pieces of eight and the other rarer Spanish coins, some scattered around the beach but most in a rough cluster that ran from the shoreline up to the base of the cliff.

At the base of the cliff, what had, from the *Meandering Manatee*, looked like crevasses now revealed themselves to be caves, cut into the cliff by years upon years of erosion.

It occurred to Chris that a graduate student who really was studying coastal erosion would be fascinated by the caves they were puzzling over, and that a graduate student who really was studying coastal erosion would also be a lot of help in this situation. The universe was funny sometimes.

"Okay, now what?" Carrie asked when they'd scrambled up the slight incline and avoided a nest of irritable ants and were all standing in front of the three largest and most tempting cave openings. "Eeny, meeny, miny, mo?"

The wind picked up. Suddenly, it became

obvious why the caves in the area were called the "screaming" caves and why people might think the place was haunted.

"Did you hear that?" Detective Hermann asked when the first gust had passed and the moaning from the caves had died down to a whimper. It was still creepy. Chris had heard the wind blowing through all sorts of old buildings but it was usually a low moaning. These caves moaned and screamed in a higher pitch.

"I can't believe you don't hear this in the middle of town," Chris said, wandering closer to try to get a good look inside. Were they *sure* there weren't any Skunk Apes in the area?

"No, I meant that chiming noise," the detective said, turning in a circle with a frown, just as Chris noticed something carved into the side of the mouth of one of the caves, and wandered closer to look. Someone had chipped the letter R into the side of the cave, and recently too, because the chips in the rock were still pale from lack of weathering, and when Chris ran a finger across the carving the edges were still sharp.

"'R' what?" Chris muttered thoughtfully. "R. Rrrr. Arrr? Are we looking for pirates?"

He didn't find any pirates, but he did find, when he wandered over to the cave next to what he decided to call "Cave R" and then again to the cave beyond that, a D and a M carved into each mouth. RDM? What did that mean? There were hardly enough letters to even *start* figuring out a cypher, and then what three-letter word could be decoded from RDM even if you did manage to figure out the key to the cypher? He was missing something.

"Chris!" Maddison said, skidding around the corner and almost crashing into him. "Come *here*, Detective Hermann's found something!"

"And I have no idea what it is I've found," Detective Hermann said when Maddison dragged Chris up a short incline to where the trees started popping up. Carrie, Redd, Bethy, Maria, and Dr. McRae were already clustered around one of the trees, a short pine with a wind chime hanging from one of the scraggly branches at the top.

"Wind chime," Chris said, staring at the object tinkling in the wind. It was handmade, just three copper pipes of different lengths suspended from a wire frame and swaying in the wind. "*Oh-kay*, that's a new and unexpected development. Who leaves wind chimes on deserted beaches?"

"Who *makes* wind chimes and leaves them on deserted beaches?" Maddison added, reaching out and grabbing one of the chimes. "It's actually kind of pretty in a really understated way—huh."

"What's 'huh'?" Chris asked. In his experience someone stopping halfway through a sentence to go "huh," usually meant that something shocking had just been discovered. And from the way Dr. McRae was suddenly looking interested and concerned, Maddison's father felt the same way.

"There's a number on this chime," Maddison said. "And on this one," she added, dropping that chime and snagging another as the whole wind chime tried to revolve away in a light wind. "And I'm willing to bet that there is also . . . "

"A number on this one," Carrie finished, tapping it. "This is wind chime number three. Two and one?" she pointed to Maddison's chime and the one floating free. Maddison nodded.

"There are three caves back there with letters carved into the entrances," Chris offered. "R, D, and M."

"Not ABC?" Maddison asked.

"Nope," Chris said. "Do the letters RDM mean anything to you?" Maddison shook her head. So did Carrie, Bethy, Maria, Redd, Detective Hermann, and Dr. McRae, although Detective Hermann shook his head slowly and thoughtfully, like he was reserving judgement for the time being.

"I guess it could be someone's initials," Carrie offered dubiously.

"But why put them on wind chimes?" Maddison asked. She was still turning one of the chimes over in her hand, and suddenly froze. "Plus, this one has a star on it."

That did not help matters. It was abundantly clear that this was a clue to which cave they needed to go into, hopefully a clue to which cave had the treasures of the *San Telmo* buried in its depths, *hopefully* left by someone on their side—but what connection could there possibly be between a wind chime and the letters RDM? They tried rearranging the letters in a handful of ways, went back to the wind chimes themselves a second time, and even walked down to the caves again, but nothing jumped out at Chris.

"What do you think?" Maddison asked her dad after counting the number of tips on the star she'd discovered didn't go anywhere.

"I think I miss Ryan," Dr. McRae said. "I'm good at codes and cyphers; he was much better at the whole 'cross-discipline' thing." He flicked one of the chimes absentmindedly, and then squinted in concentration as it rang out. "I doubt it's relevant, and my ear isn't the best," he said, "but these have a really good tone, don't they?"

Detective Hermann dropped the doubloon he was fiddling with. "Oh," the detective said. "I was thinking it was just a flight of fancy. Do you mind doing that again?" Dr. McRae raised an eyebrow but he flicked the chime again. Then he did the same thing to one and then the other of the chimes, everyone watching Detective Hermann intently as he did. The detective tilted his head and nodded, and when the last of the ringing had faded out he said, "*Do*, *re*, and *mi*."

"*Really?*" Maddison yelped.

"It's a scale?" Chris asked. Also, was that "re" like in Mc*Rae*, and so a secretive message from Aunt Elsie, or was he reading too much into things?

"Do that again and let me get it on camera," Bethy said.

"Those chimes do have a really clear tone," Detective Hermann said, "and they're each a tone on a scale. So, *do*, *re*, *mi*, one, two, three—which chime has a star on it again?"

"Number two," Maddison said.

"Well that makes it even easier," Dr. McRae said. "We don't have to figure out if the scale is supposed to be descending or ascending, we know *re* is in the middle either way."

"Unless this is a trick to throw us off the track," Chris said, suddenly worried. He didn't have an ear for music; Carrie had done piano lessons in elementary school but Chris had never been interested. He would never have figured out what the wind chimes were supposed to tell him if they hadn't brought Detective Hermann along. And if the person who'd gotten this far before them (but not too far before them) had been Aunt Elsie, then why would she leave a clue that Chris didn't have a hope of figuring out, and Carrie very little?

"I don't think this is a trick," Redd said. He shared a look with Dr. McRae, who nodded. They both looked much more somber than two people looking for buried treasure had any right to look, especially since if Detective Hermann was right they'd all just gotten one step closer to finding the *San Telmo*. "Ryan Moore was a halfway-decent saxophone player," Redd said, "and what he was lacking in real talent he made up for with practice and determination. He'd have figured this clue out in a heartbeat, and Elsie would know that one of us would know that she'd be thinking of him right about now."

"If that sentence made sense, which it really didn't," Dr. McRae sighed, "this was most likely a clue meant for me or Redd, or even for Griffin," he clarified. "And knowing Elsie, she also did this specifically to remind everyone of Ryan and to make sure that if any one of us had a guilty conscience, he would suffer going forward."

On the one hand, that was reassuring. And if Redd and Dr. McRae were right, then they were safely one step closer to the *San Telmo* and Aunt Elsie had left them one last clue. On the other hand,

Chris couldn't help feel like the caves were darker and creepier now that Aunt Elsie had reminded them of Ryan Moore. It was like she'd come back from beyond the grave to remind them that *she* was beyond the grave—and going into a cave, underground, to the *underworld*, just after talking about a guilty conscience, was a little too metaphorical for Chris.

And did the mouth of the cave have to have so many teeth-like edges?

"Chris, stop daydreaming and come on," Carrie said, rapping gently on his head with her flashlight. "We still have to find this ship." And she led the way into the mouth of the cave marked "R."

CHAPTER FIVE

IT WAS DARK INSIDE, AND EVEN DAMPER AND MORE humid than it was outside, and the one saving grace was that there did not appear to be any bats. Chris swept his flashlight across the ceiling looking for them before it occurred to him that a bright beam of light might wake up and startle a ceiling full of bats, which was not conducive to a bat-free existence.

And maybe there were so few bats because there was so much water. The screaming caves were, after all, sea caves, and they had been carved out of the white limestone cliffs by centuries of pounding waves, and something of the ocean still soaked through the very rock. They had water-worn walls and floors gritty with sand and shells, seawater pooled in depressions on the floor or running in small streams through the caves, on the way from one mysterious underwater river to another.

The cave Aunt Elsie had carved an "R" into had a wide opening, which led into a winding tunnel through which the wind screamed at odd intervals. For the first couple of yards they even had a little natural light to offset the flashlights they soon had to switch on, along with Maddison's headlamp. Then the cave narrowed and sloped downward a bit and the walls got closer, and they came to their first problem.

"Two different branches," Redd said, halting in front of them. "Should we flip one of the pieces of eight?" They had packed all the coins, as well as the modern coins and the car key, into paper-towel-lined plastic bags. Chris had only gotten a moderate number of alarmed looks when he'd produced the bags. "It pays to be prepared," he'd insisted.

"We have enough people to split into two groups," Carrie pointed out, and Redd grimaced. "I don't want to either, but unless we—what is it, Maddison?" Maddison was frowning intently at the ground by their feet, and when Carrie asked, she knelt down and scooped something up from the floor.

"It's your necklace," she said to Carrie, whose hand immediately flew to her throat, where she'd been wearing her aunt's locket the way she almost always did.

"I'm still wearing my necklace," Carrie said, bewildered.

"Well, then, this is an excellent copy," Maddison said.

She rubbed a bit of sand from the face of the object in her hands and held it out to Carrie, who said, "What on Earth?" and continued to stare. Chris leaned over Carrie's shoulder. Resting in

Maddison's palm was a compass, only a little bigger than Carrie's necklace and the exact same shape and bronze color.

"I found it lying on the ground next to this branch of the tunnel," Maddison said, turning it over so Chris could see the back and then handing it to Detective Hermann, who was stuck at the back of their little adventuring party because he was bringing up the rear in case of unexpected Griffins. "It looks almost exactly like the necklace your aunt gave you but I think it was supposed to be a working compass," Maddison said.

Detective Hermann passed the compass to Dr. McRae, who looked at it and gasped.

"Mads," he asked, squeezing the compass to death in a fist, "did you find it lying randomly on the floor, or was it propped up?"

"It was leaning against the wall where I could see it," Maddison said. "Dad, what's the matter?"

"We could never get it to work," Dr. McRae said

to himself. "This—it was supposed to be a working compass when Ryan gave it to Elsie."

"Wait, *what?*" Chris yelped.

"Aunt Elsie never explained where she got this necklace from," Carrie told Dr. McRae. "Just that it was very special to her."

"Ryan bought the locket for Elsie the summer before everything went wrong," Dr. McRae said, looking sadly at the compass. "He had a friend who worked at a small, family-owned metalworking business and he did all of the detail work for next to nothing because Ryan made him a pie. Elsie had always wanted a locket-type necklace that wasn't a heart or an oval. The compass—the compass was an afterthought and it never really worked, there was something wrong with the inner mechanisms and it stopped being able to point north three days after Elsie got it."

"So, what is it doing *here?*" Chris demanded, even though he already knew.

"Elsie didn't exactly lose the compass after it

stopped working," Dr. McRae said. He rubbed the last of the grit from the face of the compass and handed it to Carrie, who stuffed it hurriedly into a pocket. "She just used it as a paperweight."

"But she never forgot it was a compass." Redd sounded delighted. "And what good is a compass if you can't use it to point the way?"

"So, then she used it as a trail marker," Carrie said. "To let us know which way she went when she was here." She was trying to peer around Chris and down the tunnel. The cave they were in had hardly hit claustrophobic levels of narrowness and low ceilings, but only two people could walk comfortably side by side, and turning around when you'd stopped suddenly was an upright version of Twister. And the caves were living up to the "screaming" part of their name by screaming off and on with no warning, in a horrible, high-pitched tone that made everyone jump. "But a trail marker to what?"

"I guess we take this branch and go find out," Chris said. Then he almost ran into Maddison and nearly tripped Carrie. The cave was getting narrower. It continued to get narrower as they went along, the rock walls they were passing a slightly different color and a harder type of sandstone, and then finally it opened out again, into an echoing cavern flooded with water and very faintly lit with natural light from some access point far above.

"Hello," Redd said as he popped out of the doorway. "Mysterious cavern ahoy!"

"Huh," said Chris, who was picking his way on partially and only just submerged rocks to where the water in the cavern looked deeper, shining his flashlight into the water as he went. "I still don't see the *San Telmo*."

That was when Maria almost stepped on a sword. It had been buried in the wet sand at an angle, so when she stepped just slightly on the bent hilt it sprang out of the sand only halfway, and Maria yelped and sat down. Chris, startled, missed a step on a slippery rock and landed with a painful splash in waist-deep water.

"Mercy!" Maria gasped, digging gingerly around the banged-up metal sword until she'd dislodged the whole thing. "Is this what I think it is?"

"Ooh, a nicely preserved Spanish rapier!" Dr. McRae said, dropping to his knees next to Maria to examine it. "Err," he added guiltily, "you aren't hurt, are you?"

"It missed me," Maria said cheerfully. "But this means we're on the right track, doesn't it?"

She was tugging her fins on as she spoke, and adjusting her mask, and Chris realized what she was planning to do—take a dive into the deepest part of the underground lake—just a second before she went and did it. It should not have been possible for anyone to take what was basically a running leap at the water while loaded down with an oxygen tank and wearing flippers, but Maria managed it. Chris needed to re-evaluate his assessment of Maria as "more ordinary than Redd." She was weirder, or at least even more impulsive.

Dr. McRae appeared to share Chris's sentiment.

"Where, exactly, did you *find* her?" he asked Redd as the ripples disappeared and the water went still again.

"I told you, I was taking some filmmaking courses in Ohio," Redd explained. Dr. McRae gave him a *look*, and he grinned sheepishly and added, "We were shooting a scene at the same rock quarry her scuba-diving class was using for dive practice, and she rescued me when I fell in. We started talking about how much we didn't like cold weather and she told me to look her up the next time I was in Florida. If she'd managed to move to Florida by that point."

Dr. McRae pinched the bridge of his nose. "And it didn't occur to you that a professional scuba diver who did all her preliminary certifications in a land-locked *Midwestern* state might be a little . . . " He visibly tried to find a polite way to phrase the next bit, but couldn't. " . . . off the deep end?"

Oh, hey, that one was a pun, Chris thought.

"Ohio's not completely landlocked," Bethy

pointed out. "They have the Great Lakes along one border and a couple of rivers."

"I think Kevin is more worried about the fact that she just took off into what, for all we know, is an unexplored cave system. Without any backup, with one light, and with a single spool of bright orange nylon thread to lay a track so she doesn't get lost," Detective Hermann said. "There could be all kinds of dangers down there that we don't know about. Rock slides, strong currents, wreckage . . . "

"Really cold water," offered Chris, who was not wearing a wetsuit the way Maria was and was currently soaked up to his shoulders.

"Angry fish," Maddison offered. Several people stared at her. "What?" she asked. "I mean I was *gonna* point out that mythical lost nuclear submarine that's supposed to be around here somewhere but I figured I wouldn't alarm anyone unnecessarily."

Chris, who, now that he thought about it, did remember reading that there was supposed to have been a nuclear submarine that went missing some-where near Archer's Grove in the fifties, decided not to mention that Cesar Francisco was rumored to have made it to this end of the island before dying from his wounds.

"Angry fish *are* alarming," said Carrie, who had never forgotten their family fishing trip when they were twelve.

"There are no angry fish or nuclear submarines in this cave system," Redd said patiently, with a con-fidence that he couldn't possibly feel, as he hadn't explored the cave system himself, yet. Dr. McRae opened his mouth to say something more, probably on the subject of Ohio or unseen dangers, but then Maria broke the surface of the water with a splash.

"So, this cave system's amazing," she said as soon as her mouthpiece was out, sloshing across the cavern towards them with something bundled in her fist. "The water is almost crystal clear and it's not that cold." Chris would have disagreed with that statement but he was much too curious about what Maria was holding. "And there's natural light coming in from somewhere."

She came to a halt in front of Chris and dumped a huge fistful of coins on his lap.

"And there's this massive wreck of a ship washed up in the cavern right next to this one," she said.

CHAPTER
SIX

"You *found* it?"

"Well . . . does the *San Telmo* have a prow with an octopus on it?"

Bethy made a little yelp of triumph and Carrie and Maddison both clapped hands over their mouths in shock. Dr. McRae went white as a sheet, and Redd folded into a sitting position on the floor so quickly he must have been feeling wobbly. Chris was already sitting down—he'd never bothered to get up after falling in the water the first time—but he felt like he needed to anyway. "Where?" he whispered, and Maria looked at him in amusement.

"You can't see it from here," she explained, "but there's a trail of gold and silver coins underwater that lead from this cavern into the next. I think the water must naturally flow in through here, into the next cavern, and then back out with the tides, and I'll bet the waves get bad when it storms. Anyway"—she had noticed the rise in fidgeting and so continued—"I'll bet if you squeeze through that hole in the left wall of this cavern," she said, smiling and pointing, "you'll come out in the next one. You could probably even swim under without gear if you knew where you were going."

"I'll see if I fit through the hole first," Chris said. Getting lost underwater sounded terrifying, and he was beginning to doubt that Maria had *any* kind of a self-preservation instinct. Not that squeezing through a narrow crevice between one cave and the next was Chris's idea of fun; claustrophobia wasn't a *problem* for him but Chris could certainly see why some people had trouble with tight spaces. And being underground with the weight of most of the island pressing down on him made the mild feeling of being buried alive worse. This particular narrow crevice wasn't that bad, though. If Chris turned sideways, and didn't take deep breaths it would all be—he froze. Then backed out the three sideways steps he'd managed and turned to Dr. McRae.

"I," Chris said, "um, sorry—did you want to go first? You and Redd?"

Dr. McRae looked at the crevice for a long moment before answering, and when he did his gaze was distant. "I won't speak for Redd," he said. "We drifted too far apart too long ago for me to do that. But *I* don't. This was your idea, yours and Carrie's and Maddison's, so I want the three of you to see the *San Telmo* first. It's not my ship anymore." He paused. "But, um, maybe Detective Hermann could actually go first and take a good look around before Griffin pops out of a corner or something?"

"But Aunt Elsie," Chris said. "She was—well, she was your . . . "

"Yes," Dr. McRae said, "but she was *your* aunt."

Chris turned to Redd, who looked uncharacteristically somber himself. "I'll follow you with Bethy," he said quietly. Bethy had the video camera in her hands, and it was on—she'd been filming their meandering progress even though she'd told Redd she didn't think there would be anything useful in the resulting tape—but she currently had it pointed politely at the floor. "There are certain things that you don't exploit on television, and this is one of them," she said.

Then Carrie decided to be extra weird about it, too. Which for Carrie meant that instead of leading the way like a sensible person when Detective Hermann called back through the crevice that a grown man could fit through it, and it was all clear, she stuffed Chris into the narrow crevice ahead of her and Maddison. Chris had a feeling they had somehow discussed this beforehand because Maddison didn't seem surprised when Carrie took leave of her senses and shoved Chris in front of her, saying, "You believed in this the most, you go first."

"Okay, okay," Chris hissed, walking like a large and awkward crab. "I'll go first. Everyone's lost their marbles and I'm the only one who—*whoa.*"

He hadn't let himself daydream about what it would look like when he found the *San Telmo.* There were too many variables, there was so much danger, and Chris had never been able to shake the sneaking feeling that they would find the *San Telmo* only to discover it had already been looted and stripped of everything valuable. So, he'd never let himself think about what it would look like if (or when) he found the ship deep underwater or in pieces on a beach somewhere. Aside from reading every description of the *San Telmo* he could get his hands on—it was a very ordinary example of the typical Spanish merchant vessel of the time, distinctive only in the octopus carved on the prow—Chris had refused to let his imagination run away from him.

But if he had ever allowed himself to let his imagination wander, to picture the shattered hull and the octopus prow and the chests of treasure meant for the dowry of a princess, it would have looked a little like what he was seeing. Only not nearly as cool.

It was the most amazing thing Chris had ever seen. Shipwrecks underwater were subject to the ravages of time and saltwater; this ship had escaped much of that by washing up on land. The *San Telmo* lay on the rocky floor of the cavern, her prow with the fabled octopus crushed against the far wall of the cave and her wrecked and splintered back listing into the water. Heavy wooden chests, the iron bands and hinges that had once held them together rusting away in the damp, were scattered around the cave. The ancient lids had cracked open here and there to spill a tempting array of dirt-encrusted treasure.

And what treasure! They had been finding coins all day at a volume much greater than you *ever* got with washed-up shipwrecks, even off the Florida coast, but as Chris splashed through shallow puddles to the hull of the *San Telmo* he walked over more coins than he had ever seen in his life. It was like Aladdin's cave. There were tarnished silver plates and dimly glowing golden plates and strings and strings of beads of both gold and silver. There were strings of fat pearls. There were finely engraved silver forks and knives with pearls set in the handles, wine glasses only partly crushed, silver and gold and even ceramic candlesticks. There were plates of the finest china, their delicate patterns clear even after all these years. There were bracelets and rings, rubies and emeralds, even more pearls and the rotting remnants of bolt after bolt of fine fabric. There was, in short, a king's ransom—or perhaps more accurately a future queen's—hidden here by the Atlantic Ocean.

"This is amazing," Chris said, splashing in a circle in the shallow standing water. "And to think it was here all this time! Why didn't anyone follow the trail of coins back to this years ago?"

"People only see what they want to see," Dr. McRae said faintly. He had followed Carrie and Maddison through and was standing just out of the crevice, staring at the ship. He didn't look like he could believe they had found it either.

"Also, screaming caves," Maddison pointed out. She was hovering over one of the chests. "Do you think we should touch any of this or should we stuff everything in climate-controlled boxes and take it to a museum?"

Carrie paused in the act of picking up an especially tempting golden statue of a bird. "We probably shouldn't touch anything," she admitted. "But—pictures would be a good idea, and we can still *look*."

"Right," said Redd, who had been standing in front of the ship just staring at it, his eyes wide and a hair crazier than normal. He grabbed Bethy by the arm and gently positioned her in front of the *San Telmo*. "Bethy, this is a job for the person with a camera."

"I—I—I have no idea how to even *start* filming this!" Bethy said, clutching the camera to her chest. "This is an actual archeological find, there isn't a single thing I need to cover up with clever camera angles!"

"Maybe we should just look at it a little bit first," Redd said after an awkward pause. "Here, put the camera down on a nice dry bit of rock and see if you can find an emerald cut like an egg."

"I'm not putting this camera down! The instant I do that it's going to fall in the water," Bethy said, and took several careful steps through shin-deep water so she could film the whole front of the wrecked ship. When she went around to the back of the ship, camera still steady, Redd followed her.

There was a lot to look at; even Detective Hermann, who had not spent the summer trying to find the *San Telmo* and was only along in case Griffin showed up, was walking around the wrecked ship with an awed expression; Maria was poking around in the water. She'd come through underwater so she could rewind her emergency line and had fished up even more coins and a thin gold necklace along the way.

"You know," she said, rubbing silt off a coin, "I would *not* want to be the first person to go through these caves. You could get lost in here really easily and some of the underground currents are a little strong."

Detective Hermann stopped his circuit of the cave next to her. "Luckily for us, the person who found this ship before we did was not *you*," he said, looking up at the wrecked ship.

Maria looked up at him, startled; Chris looked at the detective in surprise, too, and actually came a step closer to the two of them, because Detective Hermann had never been anything other than polite and that was a little . . . harsh, what he had just said to Maria. But the detective and the scuba diver were half hidden behind the bulk of the ship, and if Chris got any closer they would realize he was there. And interrupting this conversation would be beyond awkward.

"I'm sorry, that came out wrong," the detective said, and Chris breathed a sigh of relief. "I knew someone who died, exploring caves," Detective Hermann explained. "You scared me a little when you took off all by yourself with only a line and one lantern."

Maria winced. "That *was* a bad idea," she said. "I'm a little too used to diving with a partner and quite honestly I forgot he didn't come along until I was already underwater, and then this cave system didn't seem that dangerous to me, so I was maybe taking more risks than I should have."

Detective Hermann cast a wary glance around the cave and said, "This cave system might very well *be* dangerous." *That* would have come across as foreboding, if Detective Hermann hadn't been sent along on this trip solely in case Professor Griffin turned up and did something dangerous.

So, of course, that was when Professor Griffin turned up and did something dangerous.

CHAPTER
SEVEN

THAT THEY MANAGED FOUR AND A HALF HOURS without Professor Griffin turning up was something of a miracle, all things considered. As Carrie pointed out later, with no small amount of suppressed fury, he had the same coordinates they did. All he actually needed to do was play around with the numbers for a while, and if you didn't pretend that they were some sort of clever cypher Carrie had put together—not an impossible theory, but one that assumed Carrie liked cyphers even more than Chris did—then you had only a limited number of ways to rearrange those numbers. Sooner or later the professor was bound to stumble across the right combination, if only by process of elimination, and so sooner or later he was going to find the *San Telmo*. The idea had really only been to get there before him.

It was an idea that had neglected one very important factor: that if they got to the *San Telmo* before Professor Griffin did, that did not mean they would *leave* the site of the *San Telmo* before Professor Griffin arrived. Which he did, wearing a crazy expression. And holding a gun.

"So!" he said, halfway through the crevice and already aiming a gun at Chris.

Chris *was* terrified, but underneath the terror a little voice was wailing, *Oh no, not again!* And another little voice was demanding to know why *he* was the one they always threatened to shoot. Several very rude words occurred to Chris and he swallowed them with difficulty. But Professor Griffin was dangerous and it wouldn't do to say anything to him that would antagonize him, even though he was perfectly capable of antagonizing himself over nothing.

"I see you've found my treasure," Professor Griffin said. He seemed calm, but his eyes were flicking from Chris to Carrie to Maddison to Dr. McRae to the ship, and although he'd started with his aim on Chris, his gun was now drifting through the air like he couldn't settle on a person to threaten. "How astute of you, I was afraid you wouldn't figure it out. I almost gave up hope when the coordinates were wrong."

"They weren't wrong," Chris said. The gun swung back to him and he winced. *Nice going, Chris, draw attention to yourself.* "They were just reversed."

"Shut *up*, Chris," Carrie hissed.

"No, no, Chris is right," Professor Griffin said. "That was rude of me. I should have tried looking at the numbers from a different angle before I discounted them as incorrect, I was just so eager . . . " He took a step closer. "I've waited so long to be the one to find this ship . . . "

"Well, I'm sorry to have to tell you this, Willis," Dr. McRae said, with enough venom in his voice that Professor Griffin actually took a step backwards in alarm, "but you *aren't* the one who found this ship." In two long strides he was standing between Professor Griffin and the *San Telmo*, his expression hurt and furious. "*Elsie* is the one who found this ship. And then Chris and Carrie and Maddison after her, and then me, and Robin, a—"

"Oh yeah, hey, long time no see!" Redd exclaimed, actually popping out from behind the *San Telmo*, despite the fact that if he'd stayed behind the ship, Professor Griffin might not even have realized he was there.

But if he hadn't popped up out of seemingly nowhere, Dr. McRae might have angrily told the professor that a producer, a police detective, and a professional scuba diver had all laid eyes on the *San Telmo* before him, and Detective Hermann would have lost the advantage of surprise. As it was, they now had the advantage of a really surprised Professor Griffin.

"Wyzowski?" he asked. "What are *you* doing here?"

"Oh, you know," Redd said, "revisiting old stomping grounds, catching up with old friends. Tried to shoot a film about the legend of Annie Six-Fingers. You know, the usual. It's been quite an adventure, the three of us haven't been in the same room together since before Ryan Moore died."

"He disappeared," Professor Griffin said. His eyes were now scanning the room in search of exits. Since the room was a cavern big enough to hold the wreck of a ship and mostly filled with a pool of saltwater with a sandy and treacherous bottom, he didn't have much luck. Aside from Maria's underwater route—treacherous even to experienced divers, as Detective Hermann had pointed out—there was only one way in or out, and that was the crevice they had all squeezed through.

"No, Ryan died," Dr. McRae said. "They pulled

his bones out of the cistern at Saint Erasmus last week—but you already knew he was in there, didn't you?"

"W—well, so do you!" Professor Griffin said frantically. "You're the one who pushed him in!"

"*Suuure* I am. By the way, how do you know he was pushed? The general consensus, until last week, was that he had been kidnapped or mugged and then dumped somewhere."

"Or abducted by aliens."

"Or, if you're Robin, abducted by aliens." Dr. McRae looked at Redd. Then he looked back at Professor Griffin and deliberately folded his arms. "That's why nobody believed you about the *San Telmo* the first time, by the way," he told Redd, as if they were having a casual chat and not being menaced by a mad gunman. "Nobody could accept the aliens long enough to think through how logical the part about the *San Telmo* was."

"It's not like it matters anyway," Professor Griffin cried hysterically, and Redd and Dr. McRae turned their attention back to the professor grudgingly. Professor Griffin took a deep breath and squared his shoulders. "Look," he said, in his very best *let's all be reasonable* voice, "we're all here now anyway, so why don't we share the credit for finding this thing? One last meeting of the Treasure Hunters Club, what do you say?"

"*Aaaahhhh*, I say, nope," Dr. McRae said.

"Nah, I'm good," Redd added. "Thanks, though," he said. "Nice of you to remember me after all these years." Later, Chris would learn that Griffin had let his correspondence with Redd taper off and stop soon after he had started graduate school and that Robin Redd had spent years worrying and wondering why.

"*What?*" Professor Griffin screamed.

"If anyone shares the discovery of the *San Telmo* it should be Chris and Carrie and Maddison," Dr. McRae said patiently. "They're the ones who put all the clues together and found this place."

This was the last straw, and it broke Professor

Griffin's hastily constructed façade of goodwill and reconciliation completely. "I can't let you do that," he cried, and put a bullet into the ceiling of the cave. Everyone flinched. Chris thought, but was never sure afterwards, that he heard the quiet click of a gun being cocked behind him, where Detective Hermann was lurking behind the *San Telmo*. "I won't let you do that!" Professor Griffin said. "I didn't kill Ryan and Elsie just to have the *San Telmo* discovered by a bunch of nosey teenagers!"

"Willis Griffin!" Detective Hermann said, rounding the wreck of the *San Telmo* with his gun out. "Drop your weapon and put your hands where I can see them. You're under arrest."

Professor Griffin gaped at the detective, all color draining from his face. Then he squeezed the trigger of his gun again, sending another bullet harmlessly into the ceiling, and lunged at Chris. Probably in the direction of the *San Telmo*, but that was also the general direction of Chris, who ducked in anticipation of an attack that never came. Professor Griffin had been only a few steps into the cave, and so he had to cross almost the whole pool of water to get to Chris—and he apparently *didn't* know that there were rocks, bits of ship, and unexpected deep chasms under the surface of the pool. He managed two steps before he caught his foot on something and tripped, cracking his head against a rock as he did so and splashing back into the water.

In the shocked aftermath, Detective Hermann said, "You get all that?" He was moving quickly toward the place where Professor Griffin had fallen as he spoke, barely splashing the water he was so careful.

"I have everything from when he walked in the room." Bethy's voice was shaky from behind the ship. "He's not getting out of this easily," she said. "We have him confessing to murder on film." Some of the tension seemed to go out of the room—Carrie gave a shaky laugh and sat down on one of the treasure chests, which looked like a brilliant idea, why didn't Chris try doing that—and Redd relaxed enough to turn an accusing glare on Dr. McRae.

"Nobody believed me when I told three different police officers about the *San Telmo* because I also suggested Ryan might have been abducted by aliens?"

"You also suggested Ryan might have been abducted by aliens," Dr. McRae repeated patiently. "Also, there was a moderate case of police corruption going on at the time, but it bears repeating: Robin, *you seriously suggested Ryan might have been abducted by aliens.*"

"Maria," Detective Hermann interrupted suddenly and sharply, "do you know how deep this trench goes?"

Maria tilted her head to one side and frowned, thinking. "Not really, I was trying *not* to get lost in the depths . . . Oh. Oh no, he didn't—" Eyes wide, she joined Detective Hermann by the spot where Professor Griffin had fallen. It was also a spot where, despite the appearance of a calm surface, there was a deep trench. There was no body, and when Maria looked inquisitively at Detective Hermann he plunged his hand into the water up past his armpit, stopping only when his nose began to get wet.

"He did," Detective Hermann said. "He *sank*. And he hit his head *hard* when he fell—if you don't mind seeing how far you can go straight down?" Maria nodded and disappeared into the water. "Not like it's going to make much difference at this point," the detective said. "There's a good chance he's taken in enough water to drown by now."

Chris couldn't quite believe it. Professor Griffin threatening them with a gun, yes; but Professor Griffin accidentally hitting his head and drowning because he fell down a chasm in an underwater cave system? It was not at all in character.

"What made the professor trip?" he asked.

They all looked at him, and then Detective Hermann felt around the silty bottom for the culprit. Eventually he held up a grimy and slightly weather-beaten tangle of gold. "It's some kind of metal circlet," he said, and Chris broke out in chills.

Of all the things to trip over.

"The golden flower crown," Maddison said. "Isn't that exactly the relic your aunt most wanted to find?"

Utterly spooked, Chris agreed that it was, and checked the shadowy corners of the cave for ghosts, just in case. He didn't believe it was her—and yet if it wasn't somehow Aunt Elsie protecting them from beyond the grave, this was one more coincidence than Chris could tolerate.

✘ ✘ ✘

Maria came back up breathless despite the fact that she had her own air supply. "The current gets really strong and the sediment's been stirred up," she said, shaking her head. "If he is down there I can't find him."

Detective Hermann sighed and thanked Maria

for her efforts, and it was a much more subdued group that made their way back out of the cave and to the *Meandering Manatee*, miraculously still exactly where they had left her. As they waded through the shallows Chris overheard the detective admit to Dr. McRae, in an undertone, that he wasn't surprised they hadn't found Professor Griffin. "Sea caves can be dangerous, and people who die in them don't often leave bodies to be buried," he said quietly, and Dr. McRae said that he was inclined to agree with him. Chris wasn't so sure.

"It's just that I don't think we're going to be safe until we see his d—his body again," he told Carrie on the trip back to harbor. "Otherwise, for all we know, the professor could still be out there somewhere, watching and biding his time."

"We don't exist in a comic book universe," Carrie pointed out. "There's no reason to think Professor Griffin could have survived. Even if he did there's certainly no reason to think he's going to bounce back from nearly drowning just so he can come after us!"

"You don't really believe that, do you?"

Carrie sighed, all the fury going out of her at once. "No," she said, "I don't, actually. But what are we supposed to do? Dredge the sea caves?"

CHAPTER EIGHT

FORREST HUNG UP THE PHONE AND ROLLED HIS shoulders with a sigh. "And the last marina is a no-go," he said. Michelle groaned and put her head down on the newspaper-covered desk.

"That makes two 'no record matches,' three 'we don't keep records,' and one 'mind your own business,' for a total of six marinas on the island and zero leads," Michelle mumbled into the business section of the newspaper.

"So, as soon as we have something to eat, we can go take a look around the three who don't keep records," Forrest said. He shifted three newspapers and a phone book out of the way before he found a local map. "And we can see if visiting in person goes over better with the 'mind your own business' marina," he added as he circled the marinas he wanted to visit. In Michelle's experience, people who told the FBI to mind its own business over the phone were even less inclined to be nice when the FBI turned up in person, but Forrest was eternally hopeful and she was too sick of doing phone calls to shoot down his hopes. And it would get them outside for a bit, doing something other than talking on the phone all day. Michelle was sick to death of phones. If she didn't have to pick one up for the rest of the evening it would be a relief.

The phone rang.

Michelle glared at it, which solved nothing, and then sighed and answered it before Forrest could panic and answer it himself. It was the phone on her desk, and therefore her responsibility.

"Agent Grey?" Detective Hermann asked. "Oh good. I was afraid you might have gone out to dinner already. Listen, we have a bit of a situation here . . ."

✗ ✗ ✗

At first, Brad thought he was staring at a corpse. Griffin had missed the arranged pickup, and Brad had been forced to hide in a tree so the lavender-and-crimson monstrosity of a passing boat didn't notice him. When he finally felt safe enough to climb out of the tree and try looking for the boat himself, he stumbled over a body lying motionless on the beach. He'd almost cut and run right then, but he had nowhere to run to and he was almost positive that the body had groaned when he tripped over it. Mostly positive. Oh *please* let it not be a dead body.

It had already been a terrible day. When Griffin had made some massive realization about what the coordinates on his little yellow sticky note meant he had gone tearing off to his boat in high spirits, but

120

by the time they rounded the jutting limestone cliffs and found the tiny bay with a boat anchored in it he had reverted to a stony silence broken only by direct instructions to Brad and mutterings of how it was *his* treasure, *his*, *his*, not theirs. Brad would happily have decked the man and made a break for it and never mind the consequences, but the professor was either too paranoid for him or perfectly aware of what Brad was planning. It was probably the latter. He couldn't have been so effective at keeping Brad from running unless he knew that was what Brad wanted to do.

Even finding a rickety ship painted purple and red floating in what passed for a bay—undeniable proof that they were hot on the trail of the Kingsolvers—hadn't seemed to lift Griffin's spirits, and when they'd discovered the footprints in the damp sand that pointed them directly after the Kingsolvers, the college professor had been too busy getting freaked out by a random set of wind chimes in a nearby tree to appreciate the stroke of luck.

Nervously, Brad poked the maybe-a-corpse. He'd almost cut and run several times today—once when Griffin announced he was going into a cave system alone and needed Brad to stay outside and keep watch; once when, not long after the professor had disappeared, he'd heard muffled gunshots and felt the ground shake; and once when the police detective *and* the Kingsolvers had come hurrying out of the cave minus Griffin and booked it to their lavender horror of a boat. Only fear had kept him hidden, first behind a pile of driftwood and then up a tree—fear of Griffin taking revenge on him for his abandonment, and fear of the charges he was going to get slapped with if the police caught him—his fingerprints were all over that first boat Griffin had crashed, and the girl's books, from where he dropped them at the library. There was even a nagging fear that they might have ticked off something supernatural.

Brad had never believed in the supernatural, unless you counted persistent fear of the thing that lived under the bed, but Griffin had progressed from jumping at shadows that were actually there to jumping at things that *weren't*, and Brad wondered if it was the work of a guilty conscience, or a psychotic break . . . or something more. Things kept going wrong for them in ways that left Griffin snarling with fury and Brad . . . unsettled. Creeped out, even. Case in point: if he wasn't dead, Griffin was out cold. And Brad was in trouble. Brad had overheard the police detective calling in a search-and-rescue team on his way out. This place was going to be crawling with police as soon as they could either get a car halfway across the island or get a boat out, and Brad did not want to be here when they did.

Griffin didn't *seem* dead, though, and he had the boat keys in his pocket, so maybe . . . Brad gingerly grabbed the professor's shoulder and gave it a firm shake. Nothing happened. Terrified but determined, Brad shook the man again, harder this time, and said, "Professor Griffin? Can you hear me?" Still nothing.

"Come on come on come *onnn*," Brad said, shaking Griffin frantically, and suddenly the man choked and gagged and started spitting out water. Some remnant of a high-school first-aid class took over and Brad rolled him over on his side so he could cough out a shocking amount of water.

"Are you okay?" Brad asked when Griffin had hauled himself into a sitting position, breathing in heavy gasps. "How did you get here? What happened? For a minute there you weren't breathing—"

"Brad," Griffin said firmly, as if he wasn't pale and soggy and sporting an impressive bruise on his forehead. There was something wrong with his eyes—one of the pupils was as tiny as a pinprick but the other looked normal. "I'm fine," he said. Which was so obviously not true Brad just gaped at him. Griffin *clearly* had a concussion.

"I don't mean physically, of course," Griffin said

in a hoarse voice. "But my mind's quite all right and we have to go now."

"Go where?" Privately, Brad thought there was something *not* quite all right with Griffin's brain, but he didn't dare mention it.

"After that ship, of course," Griffin said, dragging himself to his feet and managing—*somehow*—not to fall flat on his face. "They're on their way to announce the discovery of the *San Telmo* to the world and we've got to stop them before they do, it's imperative that I be credited with the discovery." *Aaaaaand* there was the crazy look again. "And I believe they may have caught me confessing to the murders of Elsie and Ryan on tape," Griffin added as an afterthought. Brad gulped. The professor didn't seem to notice. "Now, come," he continued, "there's a simply enormous pile of gold in it for you."

Reluctantly, Brad got to his feet and let Professor Griffin lead the way to the boat they had hidden under a draping of camouflage netting and some driftwood. Brad *didn't* want to know where the professor had found military-grade camouflage netting or why he'd ever expected to need it. As he followed he thought—but didn't dare say it out loud—that it would have been so much easier for everyone if Griffin really had been a corpse.

Detective Hermann radioed ahead to arrange for a search-and-rescue operation and for a thorough combing and cordoning off of the entire beach where the *San Telmo* lay, because even though he seemed all too afraid that Professor Griffin was lost in the underwater caves he *also* seemed to think the initial "falling-and-hitting-his-head" bit hadn't been enough to actually kill him. "And it's a lucky break for all of you," he added to the rag-tag bunch still on board the *Meandering Manatee* when he'd finished. "Since the area is technically a crime scene the police have the right to keep nosey reporters and opportunists out. The treasure trove that that ship represents might actually make it into legitimate museums instead of the hands of private collectors. No offense if any of you *are* private collectors," he added as an afterthought.

"No, we were planning on donating it to a museum," Chris said honestly, although the truth was that he hadn't ever thought that far ahead. But here he was with a handful of gold coins and smaller pieces from the *San Telmo* in a bag on his lap, brought along as irrefutable proof that they really had found the long-lost treasure ship. Chris felt both exultant and sick all at once; there was a buzzing in his ears and his stomach felt hollow.

"It's a relief," Detective Hermann said, making Chris jump a mile. The detective winced apologetically. "Sorry, didn't meant to scare you—but you've been carrying around all this stress and worry over *finding* that ship and now that you have it's like you've come down with the flu."

"Yeah," Chris said. "Is it that obvious?"

"On you? Yeah," the detective said. "But you aren't the only one. I think Dr. McRae's going to fidget off the deck if he keeps this up."

Dr. McRae did look very pale and like he didn't know what to do with himself. Carrie and Maddison had claimed the *Meandering Manatee's* cabin, and Bethy had borrowed Maria to help her film waves and Redd almost falling into them, so there was nobody on the deck but the pensive Detective Hermann and a fidgeting Dr. McRae. With nothing else to do, Chris watched Dr. McRae all the way back to civilization, during which time he: laced and unlaced his shoes three times, even though they were slip-ons with laces for show; made a friendship bracelet out of three fishing lines despite Bethy's alarmed reminder that they were only renting the boat and all supplies onboard needed to stay onboard; and rolled a quarter along the deck railing for twenty minutes until it slipped off and plopped into the water as they entered the harbor.

× × ×

It didn't surprise Brad that Griffin knew an illegal shortcut that got them back to the marina before the Kingsolvers. It did surprise him that it was over dry land. The professor docked his boat back in his registered-under-a-fake-name boathouse and they spent a dusty and hot fifteen minutes hiking through an overgrown utility easement and crossing a busy highway. At about minute ten Brad realized that Griffin had a gun, and then he realized that it was not the one the professor had started the day with. "That's my gun!" He wanted to wail, but of course he didn't, and instead cursed a lot of things inside his head. How had the professor *found* it? Brad had specifically tucked it away before leaving on this little adventure because he didn't have a license and he was afraid of getting caught with it.

When Professor Griffin explained that they were going to lie in wait for the Kingsolvers—and a Kevin

McRae and Robin Redd, who Griffin suddenly and for no reason Brad could figure out had a huge vendetta against—*under* the pier, Brad was too used to the craziness to bother worrying. They were going to die in a shootout with the police and the FBI, he could just *tell*. Brad found himself hoping, as he climbed soggily into the wooden struts that braced up the pier and hauled the professor up after him, that wherever Harvey was he was safe. He'd certainly proven himself the smarter of the two of them, running when he had the chance. Brad would happily have given himself up to the police, if he didn't think the professor would shoot him before he managed it.

Also, why the heck was Griffin so mad at a television host, if he really meant Robin Redd of *Treasure Hunter*? Brad *liked* Robin Redd's show.

"I don't like this," Agent Holland said. He was

leaning against a cement flower pot filled with red and orange blossoms, trying and failing to look natural with a snow cone and a pair of sunglasses. It was the tie that ruined it; Forrest collected painfully terrible ties and wore them so regularly they were his signature look. Frankly, Forrest just wasn't cut out for undercover work, unless the undercover role happened to need someone who looked conspicuously out of place. Michelle had always been impressed by how neatly Forrest managed to use the fact that he stood out like a sore thumb as an advantage; the reasoning was usually "he's far too *obviously* an undercover federal agent to be an undercover federal agent." But Forrest had excellent instincts; Michelle didn't put up with fools or incompetents and she had been working with Forrest for four years. If he thought there was something wrong, then there was something wrong.

Michelle took a small bite of her cherry-flavored snow cone. "What don't you like?" she asked. They had people watching the parking lots; the Coast

Guard was out on an unmarked boat; plainclothes policemen were lurking by the bathrooms and the nearby Ferris wheel. For a speedily thrown-together stakeout it was well done and thorough, you had to hand it to the Archer's Grove Police Department. They'd prepared for Griffin having someone at the marina waiting for the *Meandering Manatee*—a more easily identifiable boat Michelle had never seen, which made things easier and harder all at once—and they were even prepared for Griffin turning up himself. True, Detective Hermann half suspected that Griffin was dead, but Michelle was of the opinion that until you had the body you didn't count someone out of the equation, and even then, you had better make sure it was the *right* body.

She'd worked two mistaken-identity cases that had hinged on dental work, and in her long career had seen more than one case where someone tried to forge dental records specifically because they were the last resort when it came to identifying bodies. Humans were fickle and extremely creative creatures. But she and Forrest had been thorough and vigilant, so unless Professor Griffin was secretly a merman or in possession of a submarine Michelle didn't see how he could have slipped past them, and she said as much. Forrest's eyes narrowed as she did and then he sighed.

"I almost had it and then I lost the thought," he sighed. "I don't think we're done with Griffin," he said. "And this case keeps making the hairs on the back of my neck stand up."

"Great," Michelle said. Forrest had *instincts.* The last time something had made all the hairs on the back of his neck stand up they'd never found the wild animal doing the mauling, and someone had been shot with a silver bullet. In fact, their best suspect had been shot with a silver bullet, and Michelle knew exactly what *that* looked like. She just didn't have any proof. Which was what she had told both Forrest and the Internal Affairs people who'd been unusually interested in a case of wolf attacks and mass hysteria in Kansas. And as for *this* case . . .

"Please tell me you haven't *seen* anything." Michelle hadn't, but Michelle knew her strengths, and getting "feelings" about a case was not one of them.

"I've seen exactly what you have," Forrest said. "And the *San Telmo* isn't supposed to be haunted or cursed. I checked as soon as I found out about the ship. The only thing is"—Michelle interrupted with a groan. There was always *something*—"Robin Wyzowski says it's brought nothing but curses down upon him and all who have ever searched for it."

"Well, that's helpful," Michelle said, and hoped Forrest wasn't going to try to explain how it actually *was* helpful. Luckily, a distraction presented itself just then. "Oh hey," Michelle said, sighting a familiar purple manatee blob on the horizon. "There they are."

"Showtime," Forrest said grimly, and dumped the remnants of his snow cone in the trash.

CHAPTER NINE

THE MARINA WHERE THE *MEANDERING MANATEE* docked was not the newest or the most expensive, but rather a respectable, older institution right next to a beachfront carnival and a stretch of beach popular with the weekend crowd. It being a Saturday, both were crowded. The dock that the *Meandering Manatee* docked at was a long wooden one that had seen its share of hurricanes and subsequent repairs, and, although Chris only found this out afterwards, had once been the site of a strange and tragic sea-monster sighting. The giant serpent had reared out of the ocean and snatched away three vacationing teens in 1986, and then had never been seen again. But Chris didn't *think* that tragedy had anything to do with the accident or even the dock. There had been the usual rumors that the whole thing was a hoax, but no one had ever been sure.

The dock was not, for the record, structurally unsound. The wooden supports that held it up had been repaired a few times and they were a tangled mess as a result, which was why Professor Griffin was able to climb up in them without being seen, but the whole structure was sound as a nut. Which made what happened when Professor Griffin met the *Meandering Manatee* a tragic and *unusual* accident.

Detective Hermann was the first one off the *Meandering Manatee*, eyes alert and his hand on his gun. He was still worried about an attack on the Kingsolvers—Griffin had been working with at least two accomplices, only one of which they had in custody—and he was worried that the discovery of the *San Telmo*, if the local reporters caught wind of it, would make Chris and Carrie more of a target than ever before. He caught Agent Grey's eye as he exited the boat, then turned his attention to scanning the crowds and the boats and swimmers in the water, wishing they could have docked somewhere less public. Agent Grey had argued against doing so because they couldn't tell if Griffin had survived his fall into the caves and they didn't have the time to find a private place to dock the boat without raising a lot of attention, but it was true that trying to keep an eye out in a crowded location was worse than keeping an eye out for Griffin in a secluded location.

And it didn't occur to Detective Hermann to look down, or perhaps he would have noticed Professor Griffin clinging like a demented bat to the underside of the dock, or Brad clinging for dear life to a wooden support pillar.

Instead, Chris was the one who noticed Professor Griffin. He'd been following Detective Hermann out of the boat with all of his focus on what was under his feet, because the deck would lead to the dock which would lead to dry land. Chris's seasick-ness medication had started to wear off, and he was seriously contemplating kissing the solid ground when he finally reached it, and weighing the relief against the danger that kissing the ground might make him even more nauseous. So Chris was peer-ing between the planks of the dock, and he caught a flash of metal just a second before Professor Griffin swung himself up and over the side, knocking Detective Hermann over the side as he did.

"Oh *come on!*" Chris yelled, coming to an abrupt halt. Professor Griffin had a gun again, and Chris was the one closest to it again. This was simply not fair. And to top it all off he was more than a little seasick!

Behind Chris, Dr. McRae said "*fudge*" in a way that made it perfectly clear he meant a different word altogether, and Carrie actually did swear. Maddison said nothing at all. Chris later discov-ered that she'd done the sensible thing and dropped flat to the floor inside the cabin of the *Meandering*

Manatee so as to present as small a target as possible, and that Maria followed her lead when she realized what was going on. Redd froze just inside the cabin door with a horrified and frustrated expression. Bethy, also inside the cabin because she had been despairing over the fishing lines that Dr. McRae had turned into friendship bracelets, and so also not immediately noticeable, reportedly inched her camera up to the window and started recording. She'd already saved the previous confrontation on a flash drive that was double-bagged in two Ziplocs in her pocket.

In another life, Bethy might have made an excellent investigative journalist, although when Chris later suggested that to her all he got was a puzzled look. It had never occurred to Bethy that the skills she regularly used to make sure they didn't lose all their work when Redd fell in the river with the cameras were also useful skills if you wanted to get breaking news safely out of dangerous areas. Or the proof of a crime past a dangerous oceanography professor, as the case may be.

The dangerous oceanography professor in question paused mid-word and mid-lunge at the sight of Chris. Or rather, in surprise at what Chris said when he saw the professor. Apparently Chris yelling "Oh, *come on!*" in a mixture of fear and exasperation was not what Professor Griffin expected when he popped up out of nowhere.

"I was going to ask if you were surprised to see me," Professor Griffin said with a frown. "But from this rather angry response"—he cast a nervous look behind him but there was nothing there—"I . . . I can guess you aren't that *happy* to see me."

"Will you just go away?" Chris complained. It was probably not the best thing he could say to Professor Griffin, who kept turning up with different guns and wilder eyes, and this time had seaweed snagged in his collar and seemed to be having trouble focusing on Chris. But Chris didn't know what to do in a situation like this; he'd researched seminars on how to talk down armed shooters, but they all required you to be a police officer before you could sign up.

Professor Griffin took offense at this. "I'm not here to cause trouble," he said. "I'm here for the *San Telmo.*"

"Willis," Dr. McRae groaned. "You don't need the *San Telmo* this badly. Nobody needs to find a ship this badly."

"Who are you to tell me to give it up?" Professor Griffin snarled. "If you don't think the ship is worth a little hard work and sacrifice then why don't *you* hand it over?"

"It's not like I have the *San Telmo* in my *pocket,*" Chris said. "It's back in the cave where we left it! Nobody is handing anything over because nobody has anything to hand over!"

"Hard work and sacrifice?" Dr. McRae said. "Hard work and *sacrifice*? You *murdered* two people over this ship! You framed me for one of the murders! You wrecked Ryan's and Elsie's lives!"

"Elsie would understand!" Griffin said. He took a step closer—Chris took a step back and ran into Dr. McRae, who pushed around him to get at Professor Griffin.

"Elsie would never, *ever*, choose treasure over her friends," Dr. McRae growled. "Or are you too dim-witted to realize why she left everything to Chris and Carrie? She knew we couldn't handle it!"

For the first time Professor Griffin looked uncertain. "She—she would have told us, eventually. I just had to get there first, before she claimed everything for herself."

"Are you even listening to yourself?" Dr. McRae demanded. "Elsie? Claim the ship for herself? *She would donate everything to a museum!*"

"I did the only thing I could," Professor Griffin insisted. He didn't seem to be listening to Dr. McRae at all. "I didn't want to do it but I had to."

Suddenly, Chris noticed that the air was getting unusually cold, especially for a summer day in Florida. And the sky was a clear blue with friendly white marshmallow clouds, but the hair on the back of his neck was sticking up like they were about to have a thunderstorm.

"Kevin," Redd whispered next to Chris, "Willis, please—let me get past you," he asked Chris. "This isn't going to end well." Silently and slowly, so as not to attract attention to what they were doing, Chris let Redd edge past him out the *Meandering Manatee*'s small cabin door. Dr. McRae and Professor Griffin were too busy staring each other down to even register he was there.

"You did the unspeakable because it was *convenient*," Dr. McRae hissed. Chris couldn't actually see Dr. McRae's face at that moment, but there must have been something terrible in it because Professor Griffin actually took a step back.

"Kevin," Redd said, gently putting one hand on Dr. McRae's shoulder, making him jump. "This is going nowhere. We all need to calm down before somebody explodes." Miraculously, he actually seemed to be getting through. Dr. McRae chewed on his bottom lip and frowned at Redd, but he stopped arguing with Professor Griffin. Redd gave him an encouraging smile, and was on the verge of saying something when Professor Griffin started shrieking.

"No!" he said, dropping the gun from his shaking fingers and stumbling back a step. "No, this can't be happening!"

"You didn't realize we were talking to each other again?" Dr. McRae demanded. "Willis, do you care about *anything* other than the *San Telmo*?"

Professor Griffin was too busy shaking his head and whispering *no* over and over again to answer him. He was staring at Redd and Dr. McRae in horror—no, he was staring just past Dr. McRae and Redd in horror.

"I don't think he's seeing us anymore," Redd told Dr. McRae very quietly, just as Professor Griffin took another step backwards and the deck gave way under his feet.

He fell with a scream that cut off horribly

abruptly when he hit the ground. And this time—this time even Chris could tell that a living body didn't bend that way. A living body didn't land on the rocky shoreline with so little grace.

Dr. McRae got over his shock and hustled Chris back into the cabin of the *Meandering Manatee*, but Chris had already seen the professor clawing helplessly at the air before plummeting to his death, his face twisted with fear and his eyes still staring at a point just beyond Dr. McRae and Robin Redd.

"What just happened?" Carrie demanded when Chris all but tripped into her.

"He's dead," Chris stammered. "The deck gave way."

"*How?*"

Chris didn't know. There was no reason for the deck to give out the way it had. The boards might have been old but they were solid and sturdy, and dozens of people had tread across them that day without so much as a creak. In fact, a later investigation by the marina's insurance agency found nothing wrong with the deck, the supports, or the wood itself. The investigator made several appreciative comments about how "They don't make them like this anymore," and concluded his report with the opinion that the accident had been an act of God.

But at the time, Chris was bewildered. And he wondered. Because for just a second, when he looked over the side of the dock at Professor Griffin's body, his reflection was joined by Dr. McRae's, Robin Redd's, and two more reflections, both less distinct but still clearly visible.

One, in fact, was a silhouette Chris would recognize anywhere.

"I know it sounds crazy," he told Carrie and Maddison days later, "but it was Aunt Elsie."

Carrie thought about it for a minute and a half—Chris timed her—and finally said, "That makes sense."

"Wait, really?"

"He shouldn't have fallen through the dock the way he did," Carrie said. "I read the insurance investigator's report and the entire rest of the dock was solid? How?"

"Not an act of God but the act of a ghost," Maddison said thoughtfully.

"Two ghosts, actually," Chris said, and described the second reflection he had seen in the water, that of a dark-haired man not much older than they were. "I couldn't make out his face, but his shirt was red," he remembered. "And there was something silver on his hand, so he might have been wearing a ring? Or it was the light reflecting on the water. I didn't recognize him but he still seemed familiar."

"Ryan Moore," Maddison said, suddenly. They were meeting in Chris's bedroom again and she lunged for the desk drawer where Chris was keeping all their supplies from the *San Telmo* investigation. "Ryan Moore had an argument with his parents a week before he disappeared about his hair length," Maddison explained as she upended Chris's filing system. "It was a problem with the investigation because none of their pictures matched what he looked like when he disappeared—imagine him with longer hair," she said, shoving the missing-persons poster under Chris's nose.

"*Holy*—that's him, that's the guy I saw reflected in the water!"

"That's the guy I was dreaming about right before we found the *San Telmo*," Maddison added, and explained the dream she had nearly forgotten, of a man wearing a silver ring and conveying a great sense of unease. It had been Ryan Moore—the same Ryan Moore, it was now obvious—who had appeared to them in the cistern of St. Erasmus.

It made a grim sort of sense, if you thought about it long enough. Ryan Moore had died while looking for the *San Telmo* when a wooden support had given way and his "friend" Willis Griffin had refused to help him up, instead shoving him over the edge. Willis Griffin died when the wooden boards of a deck gave way as he tried to steal the discovery of the *San Telmo* away from its rightful holders. It did not take much imagination to see revenge long delayed and finally fulfilled.

Maddison went back to the cistern at St. Erasmus later that summer with her EMF meter and checked, and she wasn't surprised to get no anomalous readings whatsoever. The same thing happened when she went back to the dock with the EMF meter to where Professor Griffin had died; whatever ghostly presence had once been there was long gone by the time Maddison got around to looking. It was disappointing, in a way—Maddison would have liked to confirm, if just to herself, that Ryan Moore had really been there that day. But it was also a good thing. His spirit had done what it needed to do, and he was now at peace. And he wasn't the only one who'd been watching over them that day.

"Aunt Elsie was looking out for us at the site of the wreck, too," Chris realized, thinking of golden flower crowns and the danger of tripping and hitting your head in shallow water. "That crown tripping Professor Griffin was just a little too convenient."

CHAPTER
TEN

DETECTIVE HERMANN DID NOT FALL TO HIS death when Professor Griffin sent him over the edge of the dock. Instead, he landed conveniently on a latticework of boards a few feet from the same rocky shoreline that Professor Griffin later crashed into, and he spent much of the confrontation between Griffin and the crew of the *Meandering Manatee* trying and failing to untangle himself from the dock supports. At about the point Redd joined the argument he looked up from a failing effort to get a bent nail detached from his belt loop and discovered Brad, clinging to a crossbeam and whimpering in fear.

"I'll tell you whatever you want to know," the small-time crook gasped when he made eye contact with Detective Hermann. "Just get me down from here, and keep me away from him!"

"Griffin?" Detective Hermann asked, and then they both gave a start as a body crashed to the sandy shore between them. Detective Hermann peered down at Professor Griffin. Then he craned his neck up to meet the eyes of Dr. McRae and Robin Redd, and then back down to look at the body.

"Well," he said, "I think you'll be safe from Griffin from now on."

Brad risked a glance down, gulped, and screwed his eyes shut. Detective Hermann sighed. He hated it when cases ended like this; it always felt like the perpetrators got away scot-free and the victims didn't get the closure they deserved. Then again . . . there had been the same eerie feeling Detective Hermann got from graveyards hanging around this whole case, and an unnerving number of "accidents" that happened at just the right moment. And furthermore . . . Detective Hermann looked at Brad, still clinging to the underside of the dock and whimpering . . . this time, the death of the main perpetrator *didn't* mean that the secret of the *San Telmo* was lost to a watery grave.

Maddison finally got to go home just after sunset. It would have been even later, but the sheer number of police officers undercover at the marina meant that there were plenty of people on the scene. Agent Grey, in fact, had been seconds from going after Professor Griffin herself when he'd fallen, and was only relieved that she hadn't had to tackle someone off a cliff again. Forrest had reassuringly explained that the dock wasn't a cliff and that it looked like there were fewer rocks underneath the dock than there had been under that Scottish cliff, and thereby succeeded in making Brad cling more tightly to the underside of the dock while the fire department was trying to get him down.

All Maddison wanted to do was get one single good night's sleep, uninterrupted by her dad having a crisis or Chris making a discovery or someone trying to break into someone else's house. What she got, when they finally pulled into the driveway, was an unusually high number of cars in the drive.

"Please tell me you know who all these people are," Carrie begged, opening the passenger door of the car anyway. They'd vaguely planned on putting Chris and Carrie up in the spare room overnight and both Carrie and Maddison desperately needed to pee, so it wasn't as though they could just turn around and spend the night somewhere else.

"I don't think I've ever seen some of these cars in my life," Maddison admitted, but her dad was trudging grimly up the front drive and Chris had scrambled out of the car and followed him, and she had no choice but to do the same. "It can't be that bad," Maddison told Carrie, privately thinking it was a good thing Bethy and Redd had left for their hotel rooms and Maria had zipped off on her motorcycle. Maddison's dad had veered off to check the mailbox, as was his habit, and Chris got to the door first and opened it.

Then he promptly shut it again and turned around to leave.

"*Maddison*!" someone yelled from inside the house, and the door sprang back open, revealing Mr. Lyndon, retired police chief and normally an inhabitant of Nebraska.

"What are you doing here?" Maddison asked. Mr. Lyndon snagged Chris by the back of the shirt and smiled at Maddison.

"At the same time I booked your family the red-eye tickets last week, I booked myself a plane ticket for today," he explained. Maddison's dad turned away from the mailbox with a letter in his hand and froze dead in shock. Mr. Lyndon smiled at him. "I was hardly going to let Kevin go running off into massive amounts of trouble without coming to check in on him. And then I got in and you and your dad were off on a boat and your mother had invited the Kingsolvers over for coffee and moral support. What *have* you two been doing?"

"Greg," Maddison's dad said, "we found it."

"Your common sense?"

"No, the *San Telmo*," Chris said. He looked magnificently resigned, caught by Mr. Lyndon. Maddison didn't figure out why until after they'd braved going inside and she had managed to get to the bathroom, when she walked into the living room and discovered Chris sitting awkwardly next to his mom and dad.

"I may not have told my mom about the *San Telmo*," Chris told Maddison in a hushed whisper when she sat down next to him. "Or my dad. Or my aunt and uncle." He sucked in a breath. "And now they know all about it because your dad told them, and Mom wishes Professor Griffin hadn't fallen off the dock because she wanted to push him off herself, and I think that's everything you missed."

"Did they explain what they are all doing *here?*" Maddison asked. Her mom inviting Chris's mom over for coffee made a certain amount of sense, but they had somehow collected both Carrie's parents, Chris's dad, and Mr. Lyndon as well.

Chris fidgeted. "Exchanging embarrassing stories about us?"

In the end, despite what Detective Hermann had feared, the tragedy of the *San Telmo* was not swept away by time and tide and human error. Professor Willis Griffin was dead, but there was the testimony from Brad, the testimony from Harvey, and Bethy Bradlaw's videotaped recordings. Together, the body of evidence was overwhelming and condemning. True, there was nobody left to *prosecute* aside from Brad and Harvey, who had so obviously been pawns of Griffin that neither the Kingsolvers nor the McRaes even worried about taking them to trial, although both young men were so badly shaken by the experience that even if they *had* gotten off lightly they weren't inclined to step off the straight and narrow for a while. But Ryan Moore was finally laid to rest under his own name with a proper funeral, and Elsie Kingsolver's inexplicable death was explained to her family and friends.

The funeral for Professor Willis Griffin was sparsely attended. By the time his body was released, the discovery of the *San Telmo*, and the incident at the marina in which he had lost his life, were both the hottest topics in town. Everyone knew about the tragic, crazed demise of the oceanography professor. Few people wanted to be associated with him, and even fewer had any sympathy. Professor Griffin was exactly the wrong kind of publicity for an island that based its tourism around being family friendly. The only attention he got after his death was from a handful of out-of-town journalists looking for a sensational story; and they gave up pretty quickly when nobody at the college or the Edgewater Archive would talk to them. Professor Griffin had left his savings and his belongings to the oceanography department and it was Abigail, his oldest and longest-lasting graduate student, who organized the funeral and carried out his final wishes. He had no surviving family.

Chris went to the funeral. He didn't tell his parents, who were both furious with the professor and simply glad he couldn't hurt another member of the family, and he didn't tell Carrie, who'd been very quiet about Professor Griffin since he'd turned on them. But Chris had far more years of good memories than bad ones when he thought of Professor Griffin, and he couldn't move on without saying goodbye.

It was an outdoors ceremony on a rainy afternoon, and Chris was sitting in the back row spinning his umbrella from hand to hand when Carrie slid into the seat beside him.

"I think I can forgive Professor Griffin for everything except for this one thing," Carrie said without looking at Chris. "I wanted to pick him up and shake him and demand to know why he did it, and now I can't."

"I'd heard so many good things about him," Maddison agreed, sitting down on the other side of Chris. "I think I met the nice side of him exactly once, and then Dad rushed me out of there and halfway across the state and I never got to get to know him. Dad's here, by the way," she added. "But he and Redd are hiding by the pine trees right now."

Dr. McRae only stopped lurking after the ceremony. Chris went up to look at the headstone and Dr. McRae was suddenly there, hands stuffed in his pockets and umbrella dangling from one wrist.

"Did you ever read his favorite book?" Dr. McRae asked.

"*Moby-Dick*?" Chris asked. "No. I started it a couple of times but it was so long I never got far."

"Well, we always used to disagree about the

fundamental point of the book," Dr. McRae said. Chris couldn't see where on Earth this conversation was going but he listened politely all the same. Professor Griffin had been so fond of *Moby-Dick* he had named his submersible after the whale. "I said that the great white whale is unattainable," Dr. McRae explained, "and that Ahab wrecks himself with his determination to catch Moby Dick. I maintained, and still do, that that is the tragedy of the whole book. Terrible things happen to the people around Ahab, and then finally to Ahab himself, just because he couldn't stop chasing that stupid whale."

"What did Professor Griffin think about the book?" Chris asked.

"That it was about the tragedy of the rest of the world not understanding the lengths someone might have to go to in order to achieve greatness," Dr. McRae said. He pulled his hands out of his pockets only to cross them over his chest. "In retrospect, we probably should have seen that as a warning sign." Chris winced. "Anyway, he's beyond our human sensibilities now. I hope he's happy wherever he is," Dr. McRae sighed.

Chris discovered Redd lurking among the pine trees while taking a shortcut through the cemetery, and although he knew it was a solemn and sad occasion, all he could think to say when he saw Redd was, "I saw you in this same outfit at Aunt Elsie's funeral."

"It's difficult to go incognito when you have a distinctive flowing mane and trademark hats," said the television star. He was wearing a ball cap pulled low, with a dark hoodie and sunglasses to complete the picture.

"Do you know that you look like the Unabomber?" Chris asked.

"Ah, but I *don't* look like Robin Redd, star of *Treasure Hunter*!" Redd pointed out, which was true. "And this way, nobody in their right mind is going to approach me and ask for directions."

Which was also true.

When Abigail stopped by the cemetery a few

days after the funeral and walked out to Professor Griffin's grave to see that it hadn't been disturbed, she found a Spanish doubloon lying on the fresh dirt. She didn't have a photographic memory, but it looked such an awful lot like one of the doubloons they kept retrieving from the *San Telmo* that she started to pick it up to return it but then she stopped. It had so obviously been left on the grave for a reason that she didn't have the heart to bring it back to where it belonged.

Dr. Kevin McRae had a streak of loyalty running through him.

✕ ✕ ✕

Ryan Moore was finally laid to rest in a Georgia churchyard near his childhood home on a hazy July day, in a small, quiet afternoon ceremony under the willow trees.

It had taken that long to sort out red tape and hammer out time of death on the very distant chance that they decided to prosecute one of Griffin's associates for the murder of Ryan Moore. It would have taken longer but Agent Grey had finally lost her patience and marched down to the coroner's office and asked, in a voice only pretending to be polite, if they really needed to make a grieving family wait another twenty years to get some closure.

She was exaggerating on the years, but not by much, and she was scary when she wanted to be—really, she was one of those people who were always a little scary, but most people were too scared to tell her that—so Ryan Moore was finally laid to rest fifteen years after he had disappeared. His family had not wanted a media circus and they'd gone to great lengths to keep the date and time of the ceremony under wraps, and although there were two people there who were not members of the family, out of respect for the Moore family's privacy, they hung back.

Kevin McRae waited until all but one of the other mourners had left before he made his way up to the grave, hands in his pockets. There had been white roses to scatter over the coffin and he paused with his in hand.

"I'm going to be yelled at if anyone notices this," he said, and pulled something shiny out of the pocket of his suit jacket. The gold doubloon from the *San Telmo* glittered even under the overcast sky; Dr. McRae tossed it in a high arc and caught it, then knelt so he could toss the rose and coin in gently. Then he stood up at the sound of feet crunching on the gravel.

"Was that what I think it was?" Robin Redd asked.

"Depends on what you think it was," Dr. McRae said, hands back in his pockets. Redd was holding his own rose in the same hand that had his hat.

"How'd you get it past Maddison?" Redd asked. Because they didn't have the right sort of training and practice to do the hands-on work, Maddison, Chris, and Carrie were stuck on cataloging duty whenever they went down to the *San Telmo* site to help. This duty included standing watch at the door and over the six tables set up for laying out relics to prevent people from accidentally wandering off with gold coins, and Maddison had taken to that particular job with a gleeful ferocity.

"I tucked it into my pocket before I even left the cave," Dr. McRae admitted. "It's not like she pats people down before they leave."

"Huh," Redd said. He was fiddling with the decorative band on his hat; this one a somber black affair with a simple black-and-white checked band. "I just put it in my hat," he said when he'd finally worked the gold coin loose from the band.

Dr. McRae smiled despite himself. "Typical," he said, as Redd let a white rose and a second gold coin fall onto the coffin. Dr. McRae politely ignored the way Redd's eyes were watering.

"Allergies, you know," he sniffed and blew his nose in the Kleenex Dr. McRae handed him. "Now he's got two gold coins to pay for the ferry."

"Ryan was Methodist," Dr. McRae said gently. "I

don't think they believe in paying the ferry to cross over."

"Well, it can't hurt," Redd said. "And he got so close to the *San Telmo* before Willis got in the way, he deserves—he deserves something." He looked down at the coffin and swallowed. "I *hate* going to funerals."

They stood there in the slowly gathering dusk, mourning the loss of a friend for the second time, until the groundskeeper had to chase them out.

✕ ✕ ✕

The girl at the flower shop didn't even blink when Chris asked for asters, she just asked him how many flowers he wanted and if he would like to choose from one of their popular aster arrangements.

"*One of* their popular aster arrangements?" Carrie repeated incredulously when Chris climbed into the car with his bouquet. "When Detective Hermann said there was a sudden fad for asters he wasn't kidding, was he?"

"They're using them in all the displays now," Chris added, and removed the sparkly plastic wrapper so he could get at the stems. Chris had made flower chains out of clovers and dandelions since he was a kid, and he could even manage a pretty decent braided flower crown if he had a lot of free time to braid stems together, but the crowns Dr. McRae had been leaving on Aunt Elsie's grave were even more complex. Chris had spent two hours with Dr. McRae the day before practicing the technique Dr. McRae had learned from Aunt Elsie, who in turn had originally learned it from Ryan Moore's sister the summer Elsie spent in Georgia. To make this kind of flower crown you had to be able to braid with four strands and weave three different braids together, and even though Chris had practiced on a dozen crowns the day before, the one he made out of asters was still a little lopsided. Putting it on

Maddison's head only made the lopsidedness more obvious, and was that a stem sticking out?

"Chris, it's fine," Maddison said. "It looks wonderful." She'd been witness to his many failed attempts the day before.

"It looks wonderful in the car mirror," Carrie pointed out to be contrary. Maddison took the crown off her own head and placed it delicately on Carrie's. "Now my ears tickle," Carrie commented.

"Guys," Chris protested. This had seemed like a good idea last week when he proposed it but now he was getting irrationally nervous. It was just a cemetery. Nothing to be afraid of. Except the *cemetery* wasn't what was making Chris nervous.

Aunt Elsie's grave was less of a fresh wound now. The grass was strong and sturdy over it, the headstone had been rained on until it lost that new-stone look, and there was an opportunistic weed growing close up against the headstone where the lawnmower couldn't reach. Time had softened the scene, and yet it was hard to tell if seeing the hand of time was comforting or painful. All Chris knew when they reached it was that it made something ache in his heart.

"Hi," Chris said to his aunt, every single word deserting him. "Um. I brought you something different," he said, and held up the flower crown like an idiot before setting it down in front of his aunt's headstone and settling cross-legged in front of the headstone himself. After a beat, Carrie and Maddison sat down on either side of him. "Dr. McRae taught me how to make these," Chris went on. "He says you were the one who taught him. I'm not very good at it yet but I wanted to—" The tears welled up. Chris took a shuddering breath and was distantly aware of an arm around his shoulder and a Kleenex being pressed into his hand. "I figured I should let you know I met him," he managed. "And his daughter—you never met Maddison, but I think you would have liked her. She's really good at codes."

"Hi, Miss Kingsolver," Maddison said politely,

producing another Kleenex for Chris. "We wanted to thank you for leaving Chris that letter."

Carrie, who had been sitting in silence—and in fact had been very quiet most of the day—finally cleared her throat. "Also," she said, "Chris needs to tell you about how we found the *San Telmo*."

"I do? But she already knows!"

Carrie handed him another tissue. "Aunt Elsie already knew about half the stuff we got up to, but we still told her."

Chris looked at the headstone, and thought about his aunt, and sighed. "Okay, well you already know how this whole thing started," he began.

CHAPTER ELEVEN

THEY SAW THE FBI AGENTS OFF AT THE AIRPORT with homemade cookies. It was the least Chris and Carrie could do, and Maddison agreed that if nothing else, the intention would be kindly received, so they spent a day in Chris's kitchen making chocolate-chip cookies, oatmeal-raisin cookies, and chocolate-chip-oatmeal-raisin cookies—which happened when Maddison got distracted halfway through and added oatmeal to the wrong batter. They should not really have tried watching a documentary on Russian Bigfoot sightings while baking cookies, but you could almost see the television in the living room from the kitchen and they had wanted to check out Robin Redd's latest gig. Apparently, Harry Bradlaw had volunteered Redd for a low-budget documentary on Bigfoot sightings in Russia. The previously arranged star had broken a leg and so couldn't handle the terrain and the entire crew was in a panic of preparation. Redd was deeply disappointed that he might not get to help out with the *San Telmo* excavation and Bethy thought they were all going to die from exposure or Bigfoot or frosty relations between the US and Russia, and was more than half convinced her brother had arranged the ever-so-convenient broken leg.

Agent Grey was touched by the cookies, although she didn't show it much. Her partner, on the other hand, ate three of the chocolate-chip-oatmeal-raisin ones just during the five minutes they took to say goodbye. But then, Agent Holland seemed sad to be leaving, and Agent Grey wanted out of Archer's Grove as soon as possible. "This has not been fun," she said, shaking Detective Hermann's hand with the hand not holding the cookies. Agent Holland stepped lightly on her foot and she relented. "But that wasn't your fault, so I do thank you for being professional and effective. If you ever have need of us don't hesitate to call, but please never have need of us ever again."

"She means that this is a lovely community and she hopes your crime rate stays extremely low and you never have a tragedy like this ever again," Agent Holland translated as he was dragged through the entry doors of the airport.

"That's what I said, Forrest," Agent Grey said. "Oh—and this is for you three," she added, turning around just before entering the line for security. She pulled a sheet of paper from her pocket and handed it to Chris, who unfolded it to discover a printed registration document that read, "Thank you for registering for this seminar," and had login information.

"It's an online seminar," Agent Grey explained, "which isn't ideal, I know. But I know the instructor and she's very good. You three are registered; the details are on there."

It was an online seminar on how to deal with armed gunmen and hostage situations.

"How did she *know*?" Chris asked Carrie and Maddison later.

"And more importantly, why does she think we need to know this *now*?" Maddison wondered.

✗ ✗ ✗

The *San Telmo* took three months to excavate, although Dr. McRae liked to say that was only because everyone they brought in to help had to stop and sob for joy first.

"And that takes up valuable time that could be spent retrieving and cataloging the treasures," he told Chris on the occasion of the third crying graduate student, and Abigail had punched him gently on the shoulder and threatened to withhold *Moby*. She knew what she was doing—withholding *Moby* was an effective threat. They needed that submersible to scour the sections of the cave that were too deep or too tight for Maria's team of four divers. Also, although nobody ever came out and admitted it, they needed *Moby* involved in the *San Telmo* excavation because they needed Abigail involved in the *San Telmo* excavation. Chris and Carrie still felt horrible about how Professor Griffin had wrecked the college's boat and nearly wrecked *Moby*, and everyone felt guilty because Abigail's thesis advisor and mentor had gone nuts over the *San Telmo* and left her without an advisor in her last semester. She hadn't even been able to do her last bit of field work with *Moby* when she was supposed to because the college had panicked and locked the submersible away for protection.

Dr. McRae felt horrible for Abigail because he personally knew what it was like to have your academic reputation destroyed as a byproduct of one of Professor Griffin's plans, and he'd been instrumental in getting her the position, although ultimately

Abigail had been put in charge of the excavation because she was good at organizing and had a knack for finding volunteers to do the tedious sifting the excavation required. And it meant that there would be no confusing transfer of leadership if Redd or Dr. McRae had to, say, go to Russia for several months.

Redd was still supposed to be filming the second half of a season of *Treasure Hunter* prior to spending August through October in Russia hunting Bigfoot, but he dropped by whenever he could and poked things, occasionally providing unexpectedly useful random trivia. Chris, Carrie, and Maddison spent most of their time at the site of the sunken ship cleaning and cataloging the vast treasure of the *San Telmo*, which was basically an unpaid archeology internship and had the entirely unexpected benefit of finally getting Chris's mom to stop nagging him about a job. Chris thought this was a terrible moral, since he had slacked off on finding a summer job and been rewarded for it, but he'd bypassed his best chance at an actual job by skipping the interview for the bakery so he couldn't exactly complain. Carrie and Maddison had been forced to quit their job with Mrs. Hadler—the scariest school secretary imaginable—a few weeks early in order to help with the *San Telmo*, and Chris was still a little shocked they had survived that conversation. Mrs. Hadler had actually said, "Well, I think that's an *excellent* opportunity," and even dropped by the site one day to say hello, incidentally scaring Chris half to death.

Chris also spent a lot of time arguing with Carrie and Maddison about where they were going to donate the *San Telmo* and asking the grad students Abigail had recruited about their majors and getting nervous at their answers. Well, Carrie was making herself nervous about the upcoming school year by asking the grad students questions. Chris just asked every new volunteer if they were studying coastal erosion or had ever known anyone who actually studied coastal erosion. "Because I don't think anyone actually studies coastal erosion," he told Carrie when she demanded to know what he was asking everyone. "I think it's a topic Professor Griffin made up."

He almost had a heart attack when one of the infrequent volunteers looked up from the repair work she was doing to *Moby*'s camera and wanted to know what he thought was funny about coastal erosion. She then sat down and gave him a three-hour-long lecture about how interesting and important and ultimately revolutionary the study of coastal erosion was going to be. Carrie just laughed at him.

"I looked up the last time the Richard E. Emanate Collection was pulled before Bethy found the page from the manuscript," Dr. McRae said later that summer. He was leaning against the doorframe of the kitchen while Chris surreptitiously hid the maraschino cherries behind the carrots. Carrie and

Maddison were busy in Maddison's bedroom looking for a missing sweater.

Chris moved the broccoli into a better position in the vegetable drawer and didn't answer. He wasn't sure if he wanted to know or not.

"I know it doesn't really matter one way or another, not now, but I thought you'd like to know," Dr. McRae said. "Your aunt had that collection out to answer a research question for a college in New York. It was returned the day before she died."

So, the Emanate collection had probably been sitting on Aunt Elsie's desk while she'd been researching the *San Telmo*. It would have been the easiest thing in the world to remove a page from one collection and slip it into another, and in so doing hide every possible clue to the *San Telmo* from Professor Griffin. Maybe she'd even done it in a hurry, just as he was walking into the room . . . Chris wondered if that had been the one frantic moment that had warned the professor, that had doomed his aunt and started the whole thing. There was no way to tell now, and so many things he could say, and all of them stuck in his throat, so what he said was, "If I get out the chocolate-chip ice cream and offer you some are you going to be one of those horrible people who want to put maraschino cherries on it?"

It didn't surprise him at all that Dr. McRae was.

"Don't know what to do with it?" Harry Bradlaw sat up impatiently. "My dear, sweet, beautiful sister, don't be a lunatic! This is filmmaking *gold* right here!"

"Well, I know it's solid camera work," Bethy Bradlaw said dubiously. "With Griffin dead and Brad pleading guilty, there isn't a police injunction on any of the film, but Harry, this isn't the right tone for an episode of *Treasure Hunter*, not even a *special* episode."

Her brother gazed wide-eyed at her and shook his head. "And people go on and on about *me* losing touch with reality and having a nervous breakdown."

"Harry, you tried to *shoot* someone."

"Piffle," Harry said, waving his sister's objection away impatiently and masterfully ignoring the fact that he was still in a hospital being treated for a nervous breakdown. "That's beside the real point," he said as his sister scowled at him. "Which is that this, my dear sis, is an *opportunity*. The kind that wins best documentary at Sundance." Bethy opened her mouth to protest. "—Ah! No," Harry said, stopping her. "Don't tell me how it *can't* be done, just go do it. Interview Redd, and that McRae person, and get them to find some photographs of the bunch from college, and shoot some street views of the Edgewater Archive in black-and-white, and make sure you get a couple atmospheric clips of that priest fellow. And see if Flo's cousin's brother's ex-wife's niece is still doing freelance composing, this sort of thing needs a moody sort of score."

Bethy sighed and rolled her eyes and made a couple of pointed comments about how *someone* was feeling better, but she took notes too, and then went and set up interviews. The shooting schedule for *Treasure Hunter* was trashed beyond recognition anyway while they prepared to go to Russia to freeze to death and get eaten by Bigfoot.

The documentary did not win any awards at Sundance—although, much to Bethy's shock, it actually got considered—but it *did* turn into something of a cult classic, and was generally expected to stream online until the end of time. Flo's cousin's brother's ex-wife's niece (who was, in fact, still doing freelance composing, and created the entire soundtrack for the documentary that would come to be called *Curse of the San Telmo*) insisted it was because of the touching traditional song about ships lost at sea that Bethy convinced Detective Hermann to record; Detective Hermann insisted it was because of the saxophone solo they included in honor of Ryan.

They gave most of the treasure to the local museum. Or at least Chris and Carrie and Maddison tried to, after Redd refused point blank to take any shares and Dr. McRae smiled mysteriously when they offered, but the museum director stared at them in shock for ten minutes before weakly asking if they had any idea how much the treasure of the *San Telmo* would fetch on the open market.

"It's never been about the money!" Chris explained, and the museum director had sighed and insisted on negotiating a purchase agreement. "So this transaction doesn't bite us all in the butt later." She had a point, especially since Chris wanted to give the Edgewater Archive rights to the exhibit and that required a lot of paperwork and three joint board meetings. It wound up being a tidy sum in the low thousands, which was still rather less than the treasure was worth but something the museum had little difficulty paying.

"Normally we'd get a lot more resistance over the cost," the curator said, staring wide-eyed at the flower crown, "but the opportunity to have the *San Telmo* in our museum actually made two of our board members light-headed. We've gotten twice our normal number of monetary contributions for the year and it's only August, and museum attendance is through the roof. In other words," she explained, "this is the best investment we've made in years, you could have asked for hundreds of thousands and we still would have been interested in the collection."

The joint exhibition opened on a Saturday in early September. They held it at the museum, the better to show off the new permanent *San Telmo* exhibit; the Edgewater Archives' related document collections were to be returned after the month-long exhibit. To his relief, the museum and the archive had agreed *not* to make Chris, Carrie, or Maddison say anything, even though they were the most accessible guests of honor—Redd and his entire film crew were in Russia looking for Bigfoot and completely snowed in, just as Bethy had feared would happen. So Chris lurked, watching people *ooh* and *ahh* over the salvaged hull of the *San Telmo*, the mast recreated to scale, the actual octopus figurehead, and the case after case of treasure from the ship. He was hanging out by the snack table wondering if the bacon-and-peach bites were the universe's way of laughing at them all when Maddison found him.

"I know," she said when Chris showed her the bacon-and-peach bites. "I was with Dad when he noticed them, I was afraid he was going to combust from horror. Then he took a picture to text to Redd."

"Of course he did," Chris said, and gave in to curiosity long enough to try one. The bacon-and-peach bites were actually pretty good, with some kind of honey glaze over the top. Dr. McRae must be thoroughly offended. Chris didn't think he was ever going to get to the bottom of how Robin Redd and Dr. McRae felt about each other—there was no one left to ask if this was normal behavior for them—and he suspected they didn't know what they were doing half the time, either.

"Anyway," Maddison said, putting strawberries on her own plate, "I've been looking everywhere for you."

"I was behind that plastic replica of the ship for a while," Chris admitted. It was intended as a play structure for kids, but it was also a great place to people-watch, and none of the kids who'd stumbled across him had been rude enough to blow his hiding place. Chris was beyond happy right now but also beyond overwhelmed.

"Well, did you make it to the end of the exhibit yet?" Maddison asked, hauling him along in that direction as she did. "Because there's something at the end I think you need to see."

"I'm waiting until the screening to see the documentary," Chris protested. Bethy's documentary was set to be screened at the museum as soon as Bethy, Redd, and the rest of their crew got safely back from Russia, and Chris was stubbornly resisting seeing the documentary until the big event.

"It's not the documentary," Maddison sang. "It's *this*." She came to a halt just past the door to the side room, in front of the concluding statements about the exhibit—and the life-sized black-and-white image of Aunt Elsie, frozen in the act of shelving a box at Edgewater Archives.

"Oh," Chris said. Around the image were a handful of smaller pictures—Aunt Elsie in front of the archive, Aunt Elsie at a local elementary school, Aunt Elsie at eighteen, poring over a book and wearing the locket and looking so much like Carrie that it hurt.

This collection was donated and established in memory of Elsie Kingsolver, Archivist, community leader, and the first person to see the final resting place of the San Telmo, the inscription over the picture read. There was a picture of Ryan Moore in the exhibit, because Chris and Carrie and Maddison had insisted that the museum tell the *whole* story of the search for the *San Telmo*, instead of just the fun bits. Chris had been there, and in fact had been one of the loudest voices there, when they'd argued for that and got it. But that picture was over with the rest of the *San Telmo* timeline. This was different, and somehow more. Aunt Elsie was, at last, given her due credit for finding the *San Telmo*.

"Carrie came up with the idea," Maddison said. "At that board meeting you missed because of the dentist appointment. She wanted to dedicate the collection to Aunt Elsie instead of any of us and everybody agreed that was a good idea, and then Dad and Redd helped find all the pictures for this."

"This is great," Chris said, looking up at the picture of his aunt. Maddison put a friendly arm around his shoulder. "I think she really would have liked it."

"Do *you* like it?" Maddison asked.

"Better than bacon-and-peach bites," Chris said.

Maddison grimaced theatrically. "Then you better not look at the dessert table when they bring out the sheet cake and the ice cream," she said. "Dad had the last word on that and you know how he is with maraschino cherries."

"Oh no," Chris said. "Well, as long as that's the only thing I need to worry about," he added, thinking of how nice it was not to have a mystery to solve. Nice, and a little bit boring.

"About that," Maddison said, removing a toothpick from a miniature sandwich with great care.

"Maddison . . . ?"

"You didn't happen to see the exhibit on Annie Six-Fingers in the local heritage section of the museum, did you?" Maddison asked. "Because we never *did* get a clear answer on who left the first handprint we saw in the woods, and it's a little hard to tell from the black-and-white picture of the 1992 Annie Six-Fingers sighting, but that sighting happened in the exact same place we found the handprint." She looked up at Chris, her expression equal parts fascinated and guilty. "So, I was wondering . . ."

Chris felt his shoulders slump. But his mind was already running through everything he had ever read about Annie Six-Fingers, and the logistics of getting out to the woods again, and how much video cameras cost.

He sighed, but he was already fighting down a smile.

"I'll just go find Carrie then, shall I?"